RUTHERFORD,

CANINE COMIC

The Adventures of Rutherford Book 1

John V. Madormo

ZUMAYA THRESHOLDS   AUSTIN TX

2020

RUTHERFORD, CANINE COMIC
© 2020 by John Madormo
ISBN 978-1-61271-353-3
Cover art © Brad Foster
Cover design © Stephen Tiano

"Zumaya Thresholds" and the dodo logo are trademarks of Zumaya Publications LLC, Austin TX, https://www.zumayapublications.com/

Library of Congress Cataloging-in-Publication Data

Names: Madormo, John V., author.
Title: Rutherford, Canine Comic / John Madormo.
Description: Austin, TX : Zumaya Thresholds, 2017. | Series: Rutherford's comic adventures | Summary: Rutherford, a basset hound, is in a disabling accident that ends his dream of becoming a watchdog, and begins a career as a stand-up comedian but still has the urge to protect others. |
    Identifiers: LCCN 2017017387 (print) | LCCN 2017035734 (ebook) | ISBN
    9781612713540 (Electronic/Kindle) | ISBN 9781612713557 (Electronic/EPUB) |
    ISBN 9781612713533 (trade paperback : alk. paper)
Subjects: | CYAC: Adventure and adventurers--Fiction. | Comedians--Fiction. | Basset hound--Fiction. | Dogs--Fiction. | Animals with disabilities--Fiction.
Classification: LCC PZ7.M26574 (ebook) | LCC PZ7.M26574 Rut 2017 (print) |
    DDC [Fic]--dc23
LC record available at https://lccn.loc.gov/2017017387

To all of the faithful and loving canines in my life: Penny, Frank, Coach, and Rita.

Chapter 1

Canine Comic

For as long as I can remember, there was only one thing I ever wanted in life. One thing that would have made me happy and content.

All I've ever wanted was a chance to be a watchdog. A real watchdog. One who would stand guard and protect his owners from harm. One who would alert them in the event of danger. One who would save his family from a raging fire, from unwanted intruders, or from pesky squirrels and raccoons.

That's been my dream for the longest time. And someday I'll realize that goal. I just know it. You wait and see.

As each day passes, I wait for the call. Will it be today, I wonder? Or maybe tomorrow? There's nothing holding me back. I have all of the necessary qualifications—I'm fearless, hard-working, and loyal. I even meet the age requirement. In a few months, I'll be celebrating my second birthday—in people years, that is. I haven't quite figured out exactly how old that is in dog years, but as far as I'm concerned, it's nearly grown up. I like to think I'm mature enough to handle the job.

But sometimes I think I'm the only one who seems to think so. If people would just give me a chance, I could be a great watchdog.

I was telling my mother the other day about my ultimate goal in life. I can tell her anything. My mother Iris, a proud basset hound, was busy cleaning up after the puppies when I found her.

"Mom, you know what I want to be when I grow up?"

"What's that?"

"A watchdog," I said proudly.

I'll never forget her reaction. She chuckled. She actually chuckled.

"Oh, Rutherford, be serious," she said. "What do you really want to be?"

"I *am* serious. I want to be a watchdog."

She pulled me closer and licked my face. I love it when she does that. It's always so warm and cozy to lie next to her.

"Sweetheart, you're a basset hound. You're not a Doberman or a German shepherd. People don't get basset hounds for protection."

"Why not?"

She smiled weakly. "Well, we're just not built that way. Look at us—we have long bodies and short legs. We're not very strong, and we can't run fast. We just wouldn't be effective as watchdogs."

I sighed. I was hoping for a different answer.

"Rutherford, you have to accept the fact that we're here for a different reason. Mr. Davis breeds us to become the best show dogs in the state. People don't come here looking for watchdogs. They come here looking for dogs they can enter in competitions who'll someday become Best in Show."

"I know all that," I said. "But it's not good enough. I want more out of life than beauty pageants. I want to make a difference. And I just figured that becoming a watchdog would do that."

My mother nuzzled my cheek. "Son, if that's what you truly want, I'm not going to stand in your way. But it's going to be difficult to convince others that you're watchdog material."

I appreciated her support. She was trying to let me down easy—just like a mother. But I'm determined, and nothing will stop me from reaching my ultimate goal. I'm well aware it will be an uphill battle. For nearly two years, I've been passed over by people looking for a show winner, and I knew exactly why. My mother would never say it to my face, but both she and I know I'll never be Best in Show.

Not that I even wanted to.

See, I was born with a little handicap that seems to scare people away. I'm not as fast as some of the others. Big deal. How important is speed, anyway? When you're a watchdog, you don't run away. You hold your ground—and I can do that just fine. So, the fact I have one hind leg an inch shorter than the other three shouldn't mean a thing. I've learned to live with it. Why couldn't they?

Heck, I've met plenty of three-legged dogs in my time, and they do just fine. I have all four of mine. That should count for something.

But whenever families show up here and see me limp around the yard, I know what they're thinking. I can see

3

it on their faces. They know a defect like mine would never win them a dog show. So, they want nothing to do with me.

And that's fine. I've learned to handle rejection. The ones that really bug me are the folks who feel sorry for me.

"Aw, see that poor dog over there?" they say. "He's cute, but let's keep looking."

I hate that. I don't need their pity. I need a chance to show them what I can do. I'm not dog show material, but I can do other stuff—like being a watchdog—if they'd just give me the chance.

So, at the end of each day, I'm still here, and that worries me a little.

Mr. Davis is one of the best-known and most respected breeders in the state. He's in his eighties, I think; all I know is that he's been around for decades. At least, that's what I hear folks say. Mr. Davis prides himself on top quality basset hounds. He tells anyone who will listen that he raises the best show dogs in the country. Lately, I've started to worry how long he'll keep me here. If no one seems interested, will he eventually get tired of taking care of me?

What I needed was a skill—a real skill—some sort of talent to make me impossible to replace. I needed to prove to him and all the others I'm really good at something—and not just good, but the *best*. Then he'll have to keep me. Right?

Well, it made perfect sense to me.

So, I asked my mom one day if she could name one thing I did better than any of the other dogs. It took her a minute to think of something. That made me a little nervous.

"Let me see, now," she said. "It's really hard to come up with just one thing. You're so good at everything." Spoken like a true mother.

"Mom, I'm not talking about being *good* at something. Is there anything I do *better* than anyone else?"

She turned her head and smiled. Then, as it sometimes does, her back leg started thumping, and it slowly began moving in the direction of her head. I knew exactly what she needed.

"Let me take care of that for you," I said. "That's what I'm here for." I reached up with my front paw and began scratching her ear.

"Mmmmm." She put her head back and closed her eyes. "Now, *there's* something you're really good at."

"Anybody can scratch an itch," I said. "There's gotta be something better."

My mother was now in deep thought. "Give me another minute."

This wasn't going well. If your own mother couldn't think of something—anything—that set you apart from the pack, then you were in big trouble.

She looked at me with a nervous smile. I could tell she was struggling to come up with something. It was starting to get embarrassing—for both of us. It was time to change the subject.

"Hey, Mom, did you hear about the dog who got too close to an electric fan and lost his nose?"

"Oh, dear," she said. "Without a nose, how does he smell?"

I grinned. "He smells like all dogs—awful!"

She shook her head and started laughing. "Oh, Rutherford, where do you come up with this stuff? You never seem to run out of…" She paused. "Wait a minute. That's it."

"What?" I said.

"You're the best joke-teller on the farm—hands down."

I smiled. You know, she was right. As much as I've always wanted to be someone's watchdog, I kind of knew it might take time to get discovered. And so, just to keep my spirits up, and to make the others think I was okay with being passed over, I went out of my way to learn new jokes to tell everyone.

It always made me feel good to see the others laugh. It took some of the sting out of rejection. And when I stopped to think about it, no one knew more jokes than I did—and if I have to say so myself—no one could deliver a punchline any better than I can. It's an art, I'll have you know. And it all has to do with timing.

"I do like telling a good joke," I said. "And all the others do seem to enjoy them."

"They love your jokes," my mother said. "You have a real talent, son."

It was nice to hear her say that. So, I *could* do something better than the rest. That was great.

But the more I thought about this talent of mine, the more I wondered how it would help me in the long run. I was flattered that other dogs enjoyed my humor, but was it enough to convince Mr. Davis I was a valuable asset here on the farm?

"I like entertaining everyone," I told my mother, "but what good is it, really?"

"What good is it?" she said. "Rutherford, you single-handedly keep the morale sky-high around here. Everyone is always so happy to see you. You're never without a smile and a funny story. That's priceless."

"But Mr. Davis is a human. He can't understand my jokes. He doesn't know I have this talent. Someday, he's going to get tired of taking care of me, and he's just going to dump me somewhere."

My mother shook her head. "What are you talking about? Mr. Davis loves you. He knows that you're…" She glanced at my short leg, "…special. He would never get rid of you. You're one of his favorites." She smiled weakly. "Of course, I wish I could say the same thing about his son."

His son—now, that was another subject. Horace Davis was nothing like his father. He always seemed to be in a foul mood. He never played with any of us. I don't think he even liked us. He treated us like—well, dogs. And he never smiled.

Wait a minute—I take that back. Whenever someone pulled out his wallet to pay for one of us—then, and only then, would he smile.

I, for one, didn't trust him. And I'm sure my mother felt the same way. More than once she warned us about staying away from him. I wasn't sure why, but I didn't want to find out.

He always made me feel uncomfortable. Whenever he saw me, he would shake his head and make this grunting sound. For the longest time, I've had a feeling that if Horace is ever running this place, there'll be no room around here for me.

I decided that if I concentrated on my joke-telling and helped keep spirits high around the place, I could survive anything.

I went off by myself and tried to think of funny situations a dog might find himself in. Then, I worked them into a joke. I recalled when a family with a bunch of kids came by one time. The kids were chasing some of the dogs and teasing them. I thought of a good one.

Hey, what's got four legs and an arm? Give up? A Rottweiler in a crowd.

I'm not sure whether or not humans would appreciate it, but since they couldn't understand me, I've never worried much about it. If I can get a fellow canine to laugh, I was in my glory. I'd forget about whatever was bothering me.

🐾 🐾 🐾

After that, when I wasn't thinking up new jokes or telling them, I would play with my brothers and sisters. There weren't any of them my age. When I was born, there were seven of us, but they're all long gone now. We only had three or four months together before they went off to new homes. As hard as it was to see them go, I was happy for them. It was their destiny to become part of a loving family, and to compete proudly at dog shows. I tried not to think about it too much. It always made me kind of sad—not the dog show part, but the new-family part.

I was okay, though. New pups are fun to be around—most of the time. Humans think puppies are so darn cute, and I wouldn't necessarily disagree with that. But there's one thing about puppies that isn't particularly attractive. Have you ever noticed that it's all about *them*?

I'm not saying they're selfish. It's just that their basic instincts early on are to be individuals, not team players. I don't blame them. They can't help themselves. They want everyone to do things for them. "Rutherford, get me this. Rutherford, I'm hungry. Rutherford, can you scratch my ear?" They haven't figured out yet that their mission in life is to serve.

What really bugs me, though, sometimes, is that most of them are just too immature to appreciate my humor. I remember one time when I asked them, "Hey, how does your owner know if you've been drinking from the toilet?"

They just scratched their heads.

"'Cause your breath smells…better."

A lot of the older dogs roar at that one, but not the puppies. I guess they haven't had enough life experience.

But someday, they'll think back to that joke, and out of nowhere, they'll just start laughing. I probably won't be there to see it, but that's okay. I take comfort in the fact that, whenever or wherever it happens, they might think fondly of their big brother.

I still believed my dream of becoming a watchdog would come true someday, but in the meantime, I guess stand-up comic would have to do. And I was pretty certain I could make it work.

So, if I couldn't offer protection, then I would become the best stand-up comedian I could be. Entertaining your fellow man—er, dog—might not seem like a noble effort. But, you know, you just can't put a price on what a smile or a chuckle or a good belly laugh can do for a fellow canine. It can help them forget their troubles. I was happy to accept this new challenge.

From that point on, I held my head high, sat up on my hind legs, and was proud to call myself Rutherford—Canine Comic.

Chapter 2

Down and Out

I was rudely awakened from a sound sleep by the shrieks of my little sister Daphne. She was standing in the open doorway of the barn.

"Rutherford," she said, "wake up. There's something going on."

"What are you talking about?"

"Look out there. See that car with the red light on top of it? What is that?"

I got up, walked over, and took a look. "That's an ambulance," I said.

"What's that?" she said.

I remembered the only other time I could recall seeing an ambulance. It was when old Mr. Davis had suffered a heart attack. We were all really worried about him, but he managed to pull through, and was back on his feet in no time. That was about a year ago.

"An ambulance is a car that takes sick people to the hospital," I said.

"What's a hospital?" Daphne asked.

Here we go again. These puppies don't know anything.

The ambulance had pulled right up to the front door of the house. The light on its roof was spinning, but the siren was off. Nothing else was going on.

"A hospital is a place where they take care of sick people," I said.

"Who do you suppose is sick?" she asked.

"It's gotta be Mr. Davis."

Who else could it be? His wife had passed away before I was born. My mother used to talk about her sometimes. She really missed her. After that happened, everyone thought Mr. Davis might sell his breeding business, but in time, he decided to keep it running. I was sure glad about that.

"I'll be right back," I told Daphne. I looked around for my mother. I found her in a corner of the barn nursing some of the other puppies.

"Good morning, Rutherford," she said. "Why the long face?"

"What's happening out there?" I asked. "Is it Mr. Davis?"

My mom nodded. "It's his heart again. I've been worried about him lately. For the past couple of weeks, he's been moving around more slowly. And he looked pale to me the other day."

"You never said anything."

"I didn't want to worry you," she said. "None of us wants to think about what this place would be like without him."

She was right. I didn't want to think about it. I decided to check things out for myself.

I left the barn and walked up to where the ambulance was parked. Just as I got there, the front door of the house swung open. Paramedics wheeled a cart out onto the porch. Mr. Davis was lying on the cart. His eyes were closed. There was a long skinny tube attached to his arm, and one of the people was holding a plastic mask over his nose and mouth.

Horace Davis followed them to the ambulance. He watched as they slid the cart into the back.

"I'll follow you over there," he said.

I stared at Horace. I couldn't bear the thought of him taking over this place.

"What are you lookin' at, freak?" he said to me. He sneered and walked to the garage.

I watched the ambulance race down the dirt driveway. It was the last time I ever saw Mr. Davis.

🐾 🐾 🐾

The funeral was held a few days later. The procession drove by the farm that morning. My mother insisted we all stand on the side of the road and bark as the cars drove by. It was our own personal tribute to the man who had raised us and cared for us.

That day was a long one. Horace hadn't fed us. The puppies were fine. They still had mother's milk. We wondered if there would be more days like this one.

But to our surprise, in the days that followed, Horace never forgot to feed us once. I hoped it meant he had turned over a new leaf, but my mother set me straight.

"He hasn't changed a bit," she said. "He knows you can't sell a dog with its ribs sticking out."

She was right. We were fed each day, but we didn't get the attention dogs crave. He couldn't have cared less about us. All we were to him were dollar signs.

The place was filthy most of the time. Horace would only clean it up when he knew a buyer was coming through. Spirits were getting low. It had become more important than ever for me to concentrate on producing some sensational new material—great jokes that would take our minds off of our new living conditions.

On a Saturday night about two weeks following the funeral, my mom, my brothers and sisters, and some of the other basset hound families gathered in a corner of the barn for my performance.

"Hey, did you hear the one about the dog who went to the flea circus? Wouldn't you know it—he stole the show."

It was followed by a timely rim shot. I had taught Daphne how to make that sound. She held a stick in her mouth and banged it on the bottom of a coffee can for the intended effect. It wasn't perfect, but it did the trick.

Sometimes you have to remind your audience that you just delivered the punch line. That's where Daphne came in. The older dogs always knew when to laugh. It was those darn puppies who were clueless. Every so often I thought it might be a good idea to install an applause sign just for them. They were that dense.

I ended the show with one of my favorites.

"Hey, here's one for all you wranglers out there. Did you hear about the dog who limped into town one day? His foot was all bandaged up. The sheriff walked up to him and said, 'Howdy, stranger, what brings you to Dodge?' The dog held up his injured foot and said, 'I'm looking for the man who shot my pa.'"

Rim shot. Thanks, Daphne.

Roars of laughter were followed by applause. It had been a good night.

Barney, one of the grown-up male dogs, slapped me on the back. "I gotta tell you, Rutherford, you never disappoint." It was high praise coming from one of the veterans.

"Thanks, sir, I appreciate it," I said.

"So, when's your next performance?" he asked.

"I'm not really certain. I'll have to get to work on some new material."

"Well, you be sure to let me know, you hear?" he said.

"I will. I promise."

Barney turned to rejoin the others, but then he stopped abruptly. He leaned in, as if he only wanted me to hear what he was about to say.

"Kid, let me give you a little advice." He looked around to make sure we were still alone. "Things are different around here now. You gotta look over your shoulder at all times. Do you know what I'm trying to say?"

"I'm not sure," I said. But I knew exactly what he was talking about.

Barney lowered his voice even more. "I don't trust Horace. Nobody around here does. He could start cleaning house any time now. No one is safe. Heck, I'm getting up in years. He may have no use for *me* soon." He had a serious look on his face. "Just be careful out there, okay?"

I nodded.

"Good boy," Barney said. He winked and joined the other members of his family.

Daphne ran up smiling. "You were great tonight, Rutherford. The crowd loved you."

"Thanks," I said with a forced smile.

"What's wrong?" she said. "You don't look very happy. Did I make a mistake with the drum or something?"

"No, you did just great. And let me tell you—you have a real musical flair."

She grinned.

"Listen," I said, "I have to be somewhere. You better go back with Mom and the others. I'll see you later."

She scampered off.

I really had no place to be. I just wanted to be alone. I decided to walk around in the barnyard for a while to think things through.

I guess I wasn't completely surprised to hear what Barney had said. I had known that if Horace was ever in charge my days around here would be numbered. To him, I was just another mouth to feed. And since no families seemed interested in taking me home with them anytime soon, he was getting nothing in return.

I wandered into the garage, pushed a stepstool up to the back of a pickup truck, and hopped up onto the bed. Horace had returned from town a few minutes earlier, so the back of the truck was still warm. It was time for bed, my favorite time of the day. There was nothing like settling down for the night and a few Zs. If you never noticed, we dogs do love our sleep.

I rolled over onto my side—my favorite position—stretched out my legs, and was soon in dreamland.

🐾 🐾 🐾

About an hour or so later, when I woke up, I could tell by my surroundings that life as I had known it was about to change. I was still in the back of the pickup, but it was moving. We were traveling on an old dirt road that seemed unfamiliar. I peeked through the back window to see into the cab of the truck. Horace was at the wheel.

A moment later, we turned off the road into a wooded area. The ride for the next mile or two was bumpy and uncomfortable. I couldn't maintain my balance for more than a few seconds without falling over and being tossed from side to side. I had no idea where we were headed, and I didn't know what was waiting for me once we got there.

It didn't take more than few minutes longer for me to find out. The truck came to an abrupt stop. I slid forward and hit my head on the back of the cab. I got to my feet and looked around—trees, trees, and more trees. It was dark—really dark. The only light came from the headlights on the pickup.

The driver's door opened, and Horace stepped out.

"This is the end of the line, pal," he said. He walked around and opened the tailgate. "Well, don't just stand there," he yelled. "Get out!"

Not only had Horace known I was there, I had apparently done him a huge favor when I decided to seek out a little warmth and hopped into the back of the truck.

"Let's go, let's go," he said impatiently.

I knew that if I decided to stay put, he would just drag me out. I reluctantly hopped down onto the dirt. I looked up at Horace. I couldn't believe what he was doing. Was he actually abandoning me like this?

I did my best to make eye contact with him.

"Don't look at me like that," he said. "You knew this day was coming. What do you expect? You're worthless. Why my dad ever kept you around as long as he did, I'll never know."

I stared a hole right through him. I wasn't going to make this easy for him. Maybe if I looked pathetic enough, he might change his mind about leaving me out here.

Yeah, right.

"What are you waiting for?" he said. "Get out of here." He bent over and tried to slap me on the hind end.

Even with one bad leg, I was still faster than him. I darted to the left, and he missed. I won't repeat what he said after that. He tried to kick me. Strike two.

I knew it would be in my best interest to cut my losses and run, but I decided to give Horace something to remember me by.

Now, you have to understand that, normally, I'm considered pretty nonviolent, but I guess the wannabe watchdog inside just got the best of me. I stood my ground, bared my teeth, and growled. It was slow and deep and menacing.

Horace jumped back. "What's gotten into you?" he said.

My growl became noticeably louder.

"You're acting crazy," he said as he backpedaled.

I'll show you crazy. I leapt forward, bit down onto his pant leg, and began to gnaw on it.

Horace let out a scream. I refused to quit. I was relentless. I eventually pulled him over onto the ground.

I think it's safe to say I got his attention.

When I was sure I had made my point, I let go. He crawled away, tail between his legs (so to speak), and pulled himself into the driver's seat, fumbling for his keys. I hated to see the fun end so soon, so I jumped up against the driver's door, barking.

Horace started up the truck, put it into gear, and peeled away.

As the taillights faded into the distance, I found myself all alone with no idea of what would happen next. I had kind of enjoyed seeing the fear in Horace's eyes, but he was now free of me. He had won. My new life had begun, whether I was ready for it or not.

I thought for a minute about trying to find my way back to the farm. I figured, with my superb sense of smell, I might just have been able to do it. After all, I'm a member of the hound family. It's one of the things we do best.

But what good would it do? Horace would just find me and bring me back out here—or someplace worse. I didn't want to think about the *someplace worse*.

I looked for a place to lie down and get some sleep. Most of the ground was pretty damp, but I found a dry spot under an evergreen. I closed my eyes and tried to doze off, but it was no use. I was worried about my future.

I had no idea what was in store for me. I was on my own now. Where would I find food and water? My mother had never taught me how to fend for myself in the wild. Who in his right mind would ever expect a dog bred to compete in shows to survive on his own in the middle of nowhere?

I thought about my mom and Daphne and the others. I probably would never see them again. I knew the same thing happened when you went to live with a new owner, but this was different. I imagined Mom waking up in the morning and looking for me. She would get worried when she couldn't find me. Then she might think about it long enough and figure out what had happened.

I didn't like to think about her being sad. I thought again about trying to make it back to the farm, just to let her know I was all right. But if I managed to get caught by Horace, he might do something awful to me, and I knew Mom would never be able to handle that.

If I was going to survive out here, I needed to get some rest. Tomorrow was going to be a big day for me—the next chapter of my life. I wanted to have a clear head. I had to make good decisions.

I closed my eyes tightly and tried to imagine happier times—snuggling up to my mother, playing with my brothers and sisters, telling a killer joke and leaving the audience in stitches. Within minutes, I could feel myself relaxing. My heart wasn't racing anymore.

I tried to tune out the noises around me—the crickets, the owls, and other sounds I couldn't identify and, frankly, didn't want to. Before long, I fell fast asleep.

23

Chapter 3

Lost and Found

When I woke up, I could hear voices all around me. I was afraid to open my eyes. From the sounds of the birds overhead, I could tell it was daytime. I must have been asleep for hours. And someone was whispering just a few feet away.

"I don't know what it is," a tiny voice said.

"I sure hope he's dead," an older voice replied.

"It looks a little bit like The Demon," the tiny voice said.

"Don't even joke about something like that."

I slowly opened my eyes. I found myself nose-to-nose with something totally unexpected. I was staring into the eyes of a furry raccoon, who was sniffing me. When he saw I was awake, he jumped back, showed off his set of crooked teeth, and made a hissing sound. A younger raccoon scooted behind a hollowed-out tree stump.

"Papa, let's get out of here," the younger one said.

The older raccoon appeared to be sizing me up.

"Who are you? And what do you want?" As I got to my feet, he backed away.

"Don't be afraid," I said. "I won't hurt anybody."

"How'd you get here?" the older raccoon said.

"I was brought here…by a bad man."

The raccoon looked at me skeptically.

"It's the truth," I said. "I'm a basset hound. I'm from a breeding farm a few miles from here. People go there to buy show dogs."

The tiny raccoon stuck its head out from behind the tree stump. "So, you're a show dog?"

"Well, kind of," I said. "You see, I've got a bum leg. So, no one's ever wanted me."

"That's kind of sad." The little raccoon scampered toward me, but the older one put his arm out to hold her back.

"Not so fast, Chrissy. How do we know he's not working for The Demon?"

"He looks friendly, Papa."

"The Demon? Who's The Demon?" I said.

The older raccoon narrowed his eyes. "Don't try to tell me you've never heard of The Demon? Everybody in these woods knows about him."

"I'm telling you the truth," I said. "I've never heard of him before."

Chrissy leaned over to her father and whispered something in his ear. The older raccoon never took his eyes off me. A moment later, he stood up on his hind legs. Apparently, the interrogation wasn't over.

"What's your name?" the father raccoon said.

"Rutherford."

"So, *Rutherford,* what brings you to our little forest here?"

25

"Well, like I told you," I said, "the new breeder didn't think anyone would ever buy me, so he drove me out here last night and dumped me."

"That's terrible," Chrissy said.

"What do you intend to do now?" her father asked.

We were interrupted by the sound of flapping wings and loud quacking from overhead. A mallard duck dove down and landed on the tree stump. He stood at attention, then ducked his head and raised one foot in what looked a little like a salute.

"What's going on here, Ralph?" he asked the raccoon. "I was on a reconnaissance mission and thought I heard the sound of an intruder."

"That's exactly what you heard, Colonel," Ralph said. "This dog claims that somebody abandoned him here last night. I was trying to find out what his plans are." He looked in my direction. "So, what *are* your plans?"

"I don't have any plans," I said.

"No plans?" the duck said. "Well, don't think you can stay here. You'll have to leave. This is *our* forest. Everyone here has a job, and I'm afraid we don't have any openings. Sorry."

I didn't know what to say. All of this had happened so quickly. I knew one thing for sure—I couldn't go home. And I didn't necessarily want to stay here, but it might be nice to stick around for a few days before I decided where exactly I was headed.

"I don't know where else to go right now," I said. "Would it be okay if I stuck around here for a couple of days just to plan my next move?"

The duck slapped a big webbed foot down on the stump. "Absolutely not. We will not tolerate freeloaders."

"I'm not a freeloader," I said. "I'll work. You'll see."

"What can you do?" Ralph said. "What was your job on this farm of yours?"

My job? I wasn't expecting that question. And I wasn't sure if I should really tell them what my specialty was. I doubted if any of them would find it very impressive. Then I had an idea.

I held my head up and tried to appear confident.

"I was sort of what you'd call the official morale officer on the farm," I said.

"Morale officer?" the duck said. "Are you suggesting you're in the military? If so, you're a disgrace to the service. Where's your uniform, soldier?"

"I'm confused," Chrissy said. "What's a morale officer?"

"I can tell you that, little girl," the duck said. "A morale officer is somebody who tries to keep the troops in a good mood…to keep their spirits high." He turned to me. "So, what unit are you in? Where are you stationed?"

"Well, I'm not exactly in the service."

"How do you go about keeping morale up on a farm?" Ralph wanted to know. It seemed to be more of a challenge than a simple question.

Before I could answer, another resident of the forest appeared. A bullfrog hopped up to the group.

"Ribbit."

"Hi, Leonard," Chrissy said.

"Hi, sweetie," Leonard replied. Then he pointed at me. "What's *he* doing here?"

"He got dumped here last night," the duck said. "If you believe his story, that is."

"It's true," I said.

27

Ralph the raccoon held up his arms. "Let me handle this, guys." He turned to me. "So, about this job of yours on the farm. What did you do, exactly?"

"Well…"

Here goes nothing, I thought. I could only hope for the best.

"I'm kind of a stand-up comedian."

They all looked at each other. I could tell they were a little surprised by my answer.

"That's a job?" the duck said.

I nodded.

"A stand-up comic? Really?" Leonard the bullfrog said as he made a face. "Let's just see if he's telling the truth." He turned in my direction. "Okay, pal, make me laugh."

What? Just like that? Did he actually expect me to come up with a joke here and now?

By the looks on the faces of my interrogators, that apparently was exactly what they expected.

I immediately tried to think of a joke a frog might like. Most of my material was reserved for dogs. I had never entertained an audience quite like this before. I smiled nervously as I racked my brain for some killer material.

"I'm waiting," Leonard said.

And then all at once, it hit me. I smiled.

"Hey, did you hear about the frog who would only eat fast food?"

"No," Chrissy said.

"Whenever he went to McDonalds, he'd always order a burger and flies."

At first, there was no response. I was looking into a sea of confused faces. Where was my rimshot when I needed it? I missed Daphne.

Then, all at once Chrissy began laughing hysterically. It had taken her a few seconds to get it, but that was fine with me. Her dad caught her just as she was about to fall over.

"Not bad," Leonard said. "But I've heard better."

"Is that it?" Ralph said. "You only know frog jokes? How about raccoons?"

Oh, boy. The pressure was on now. I thought hard, but nothing was coming. I couldn't recall ever writing or even *hearing* a raccoon joke before. But I knew I needed to come up with one, and quickly. If I failed, I was sure to be banished from the forest.

And then, all at once, I got this brainstorm. Maybe I could just convert a dog joke into a raccoon joke. Heck, I had tons of dog jokes. It might just work.

But which one? Which one would make this crowd beg for more? I thought for another minute.

"So, I take it you don't know any raccoon jokes, huh?" Ralph said.

"He's no comedian," the duck said.

A second later, I had it. I imagined myself in front of a room of adoring fans.

"Hey, has this ever happened to you?" I said. "I went to the movies the other day, and this guy walks in with his pet raccoon. And wouldn't you know it, they sat down right in front of me.

"Then the strangest thing happened. During all of the sad parts of the movie, the raccoon cried his eyes out. And during the funny parts, he laughed his head off.

"Afterward, I went up to the guy and said, 'That's the most amazing thing I've ever seen. Your raccoon seemed to really enjoy the movie.'

"'It *is* amazing,' the man said. ''Cause he hated the book.'"

I glanced at the crowd, grinned, and made a rimshot sound with my mouth.

Like before, Chrissy was beside herself. This time she did fall over from laughing so hard.

Her dad was smiling. "I kind of liked that one. Got any more?"

"Wait just a minute," the duck said. "What about me? You have to tell a joke with a duck in it now."

This was one tough audience, let me tell you. I wasn't sure if I could come up with anything.

"Give me a second," I said.

"Sure," the duck said. "Take all the time you need."

I tried to imagine a funny situation that a duck might find himself in. And before long, I had something.

"I happened to be in a drugstore the other day when this duck walked in. She went right past me down the aisle.

"Now, get this—she went over to the cosmetics section, picked up a tube of lipstick, and then walked up to the front counter and set it down. As you might guess, the clerk was a little surprised to see this.

"He said, 'Just how do you intend to pay for that?' The duck looked up, smiled, and said, 'Ahh, just put it on my bill.'"

I was unprepared for the reaction that followed. The duck started laughing uncontrollably. Chrissy was already rolling on the ground. Ralph was chuckling. And even Leonard the bullfrog smiled and gave me a thumbs-up.

It was at that precise moment I knew I'd be able to stay here as long as I wanted—or until I ran out of jokes.

For the rest of the day, I hung around with my new friends. Every so often they would bug me for another joke, and I would have to explain to them that it took time to come up with new material. I promised to have something for them to hear the next day—which meant I'd have to put on my thinking cap and get to work for the remainder of the afternoon.

It was a lot of pressure, but it was certainly better than worrying about what Horace might do to me if I returned to the breeding farm. I didn't mind putting in an honest day's work if it meant feeling safe and welcome.

As nighttime drew near, most of the animals sought out shelter. The duck, whose full name I learned was Colonel Salty Quackers, slept with other members of his flock in a tiny cove of the local river. The frog found cover in a section of lily pads that floated on the water's edge. Ralph the raccoon had a special spot he retired to each evening. He had found a hole big enough for himself in the trunk of a nearby tree about thirty feet off the ground. His daughter Chrissy, however, snuggled up in the hollowed-out stump where we'd met. She was afraid of heights, so she refused to join her dad in the upper branches of his favorite maple tree.

I decided to build a bed out of dried leaves. It wasn't what you might call plush sleeping arrangements, but it was better than nothing. And if I got cold, I could just burrow into the pile. The leaves would make a nice blanket.

The sky was a little cloudy, but I was fairly certain we'd stay dry for the next few hours. I rested on my makeshift bed for the better part of an hour before falling asleep.

I still remember what I dreamt about that night—my mom. Who else? I wasn't sure if we would ever be together again, so it was really nice to see and talk to her in my dream. I remember she was just about to give me a nice piece of rawhide to chew on when I woke up. And I will never in a million years forget that wake-up call.

It came from Chrissy's direction. She had been fast asleep, but was suddenly screaming at the top of her lungs.

"Help me! Help me! Papa, help me! It's the Demon."

I immediately jumped up and looked toward the stump. It was only about twenty feet away. The clouds blocked out any chance of moonlight, I was staring into total darkness. I ran in that direction, and as I got closer, I knew exactly why she had called out. She was in danger.

In the dark, I could faintly make out a figure of some kind hovering over the stump. I could tell it wasn't a person. It actually looked like a mangy dog.

"Hey, what's going on over there?" I yelled.

The figure turned to face me. "This is none of your business," he said. "If you're smart, you'll just get out of here."

I inched closer. I could now clearly see the attacker. He had large ears and was covered in grayish-brown fur, all but his neck, which was white. He had a long snout and a black tip at the end of his tail. It didn't take me long to realize I wasn't looking at some demon. I was staring into the eyes of a coyote.

My mother had warned me about them. Coyotes were wild and dangerous. They traveled in packs at certain times of the year. So, there could be more of them out there waiting to pounce on us. I had to be careful. But more important, I had to help Chrissy.

"I have a better idea," I said. "Why don't *you* leave?"

"Who do you think you're talking to?" the coyote said. "Look at you. You're nothing but a worthless family pet. Where do *you* get off telling *me* to leave?"

Okay, apparently this guy didn't scare easily. I guess that put us at a standoff.

I wasn't sure what my next move should be. Should I stand my ground and continue to insist that he vacate the premises? Or should I rush him and hope he ran off? But what if he didn't run off? What then?

"Get out of here…now," the coyote said.

"And if I don't?"

"Then you and your little friend here are about to suffer the same fate," the coyote said. "You got it?"

Oh, I got it all right. But what was I supposed to do? Just let him make my new friend his midnight snack? I couldn't let that happen.

Chrissy poked her head out from the stump. She appeared to be okay, but her eyes were pleading for someone to come to her aid.

"You better go get some help, Rutherford," she said. "You can't beat The Demon by yourself."

The coyote smiled. "Well, at least one of you has a brain."

Chrissy was probably right, but there wasn't enough time to round up a posse. This was my battle, do or die, and I knew it.

"This is my last warning, coyote. Let her go and leave here immediately."

The coyote threw his head back and howled a laugh.

I don't remember if it was the fear in Chrissy's eyes or the coyote's overconfidence, but something stirred in me. Maybe I just wanted to prove to myself that I *was* watchdog material.

Next thing I knew, I was on a collision course with the coyote. I put my head down and ran at top speed—or as fast as a dog with a bum leg can run. It wasn't long before I hit him.

I not only managed to knock the coyote off his feet but he sailed a good five yards. Slightly dazed, he shook his head and let out a howl. I wasn't sure if he was expressing pain or trying to send some sort of message, but I figured I'd soon find out.

The commotion had awakened Chrissy's dad. I could hear him running down the maple tree. Before the coyote could climb to his feet, Ralph had crawled over to the stump, grabbed hold of Chrissy with one paw, pulled her to his chest, and was off. I watched him scamper back to the tree and scoot up to a branch that would provide safety, at least temporarily.

"Thank you, Rutherford," he yelled from above. "Now get the heck out of there…and fast."

Before I could take his advice, I learned what the coyote's howl had meant—it was a call for help. I found myself surrounded by three more bloodthirsty coyotes.

The new troops were slightly larger and a lot meaner-looking than the first one. They approached slowly and bared their teeth. The expressions on their faces suggested they were looking forward to this little encounter.

I first thought about making a mad dash, but I knew I'd never be able to outrun them. I considered talking to them, but with numbers on their side, they would never listen. It appeared that surrender was my only option. And even at that, there was no guarantee I'd come out of this alive.

The injured coyote smiled at his partners. "Enjoy your snack, guys."

Their eyes lit up. They licked their chops.

Then, just as they were about to pounce, a sound from overhead froze all of us. Ralph and Chrissy, perched thirty feet up, started making the strangest sound. They started quacking. I couldn't believe what I was hearing. Raccoons were actually making quacking sounds. And they were really loud.

"Is that supposed to scare us?" one of the coyotes said.

The others started laughing.

"Sounds like your friends are pretty mixed up," he said. "But it ain't gonna help you." He turned to his pals. "Let's get this over with."

And then, out of nowhere, help arrived. The sky was filled with the most beautiful sound—the flapping of wings. Not just a pair of wings, but dozens and dozens of them. Then I heard a quack, and another, and this time it wasn't coming from Ralph or Chrissy. These came from real ducks —hundreds of them. The noise was ear-piercing. And leading his troops into battle was a familiar face—Colonel Salty Quackers.

Before the coyotes had a chance to retreat, the ducks descended. It was one of the most impressive dive-bombings I've ever seen. They homed in on their targets, flapping and pecking and pulling and gnawing at their prey.

I just watched and admired the action. It was amazing. Then I looked up and noticed one duck hovering over me. I soon realized it was the colonel.

"Now's your chance," he said. "Get out of here."

"I don't know where to go," I said.

"Just run and run and run, and don't look back," he said. "I'm not sure how long we can hold them off." Then he smiled. "It was nice knowing you, Rutherford. Good luck."

I decided it was smart to take the advice of a wise military duck. I put my head down and started to run. After a few yards, I glanced back. The coyotes, stunned by the surprise attack, were defenseless. They snapped helplessly at their attackers, but the ducks were relentless. They had bought me enough time to make my escape.

I ran and ran. I had no idea where I was headed. I didn't know if I was traveling deeper into the forest or would soon find myself in a an area full of people. I just didn't know.

But there was one thing I did know. I was fairly certain I would never see Chrissy, Ralph, Leonard the bullfrog, or Colonel Quackers again. That made me kind of sad. But I decided I'd have to get used to that, now that I was a stray.

Chapter 4
Fight or Flight

*I had no idea where I was. I had run for miles before exhaus-*tion set in. I decided to rest for a few minutes. I didn't plan on falling asleep, but that's exactly what happened.

I must have dozed for a couple of hours. When I woke, that someone—or something—was no more than a foot away. I was afraid to open my eyes.

I had been careless. I had let my defenses down. I couldn't hear them, but my keen sense of smell clearly detected a life form of some kind. And my instincts were telling me it was a predator.

I decided to sneak a peek at the enemy and slowly opened one eye. It was still fairly dark, but I could faintly make out a figure hovering over me. I could tell it wasn't a human. It looked like a big dog.

I thought hard about my next move. If I wasn't careful, it could end up being my last. I considered playing possum, just lying there and hoping they would get bored and go away. But the watchdog in me was saying something completely different. I soon decided my only choice was the element of surprise.

I took a deep breath, counted to five, jumped to my feet, and let out a growl. It seemed to work. The figure appeared startled and backed away. In the moonlight, I could now see who it was. It was the same coyote I had tangled with before. How had he tracked me down?

"Well, look who we have here," he said with a grin.

What was I going to do? As much as I had dreamed of someday becoming a watchdog, I knew I wasn't a fighter. Even though I had helped save Chrissy, if it hadn't been for Colonel Quackers and his troops, I'm not sure what might have happened. It looked like I was about to find out what I was made of.

I wasn't looking forward to it. I was defenseless and alone. No Ralph, no Chrissy, no Leonard, no Colonel. I'm ashamed to admit I was scared.

But I couldn't show it. I knew that if your enemy detects the slightest fear, they can become ten times more dangerous. It was time for some tough talk.

"You'd better back off if you know what's good for you, pal," I said as confidently as I could. "Do yourself a favor and take a hike."

The coyote kept smiling. "That's pretty tough talk for a worthless house pet. Have you looked around lately?"

I didn't think things could get worse, but they did. I suddenly realized we weren't alone as the rest of the coyote pack emerged from the bushes.

"Look who I bumped into, boys," the first coyote said.

"I don't think we've been formally introduced," another one of them said.

"Oh, why don't we just call him *breakfast*," a third one added. They all laughed.

I needed to do something fast. I knew I was running out of time. I quickly weighed my options—fight it out, and probably be the main course. Or run for my life—and probably still be the main course. There didn't appear to be any other choices.

I was beginning to accept the fact that my life would soon be over. I was hoping the end would be quick and painless, but who was I kidding? Then again, maybe I'd just faint and never know what hit me.

I began to think about my mother and Daphne. Then my thoughts drifted to Horace. This was all his doing. It certainly looked like he had won.

And that really annoyed me. In fact, it made me so mad I made a decision. I would go down fighting. Horace was not going to win. The coyotes would eventually be victorious—I knew that. But at least they would know they had been in the fight of their lives.

"Okay, team," the first coyote said. "Let's get this over with."

"Wait a minute," I said. "Three against one is hardly a fair fight. I'd be more than happy to take you on one at a time. Unless you don't think you're tough enough."

The first coyote laughed. "Me? Not tough enough? Why, I could take you down with one paw tied behind my back."

"Okay," I said. "Take your best shot."

"You asked for it, you mangy mutt," he said.

He put his head down and charged at me. Just as impact was about to take place, I stepped to the side, and he went flying past me and into a tree.

"Why, you little…" he said as he stopped and shook his head, trying to recover.

A moment later, he rushed at me again. This time, I stood my ground. I somehow managed to stay on my feet —it helped to be heavy with a low center of gravity.

The scratching and biting began. I was careful to avoid any lethal blows. The coyote nicked me in a few places, but I kept him away from my head and neck. We were now both standing on our hind legs, locked in mortal combat.

A few feet away, the other coyotes were offering moral support for their companion.

"C'mon, finish him off," one of them yelped.

I realized that if I were somehow able to win this first match, I wasn't sure I'd have the energy to fight the other two. Still, it made no sense to worry about the next round. I had to concentrate on this one.

For a few minutes, we appeared to be at a standoff. Neither of us was making any headway. Then I thought about my heroes—all of the legions of watchdogs out there —and how they might handle a similar situation, and I imagined myself defending my very own family. At once, I felt something stirring inside me. It was a confidence and a strength I never knew I had. I began to bite and scratch my opponent without mercy.

He panted heavily and backpedaled, but I was relentless. A moment later, I managed to wrestle him onto his back. I now had him pinned. The end was near, and he knew it.

The fallen coyote threw his paws into the air.

"Okay, tough guy, you win. You made your point. The show's over."

At that moment, I wasn't quite sure what to do. I had never thought of myself as a violent creature. I just wanted to protect others. I didn't want to hurt anybody.

Then I made a choice that will forever haunt me. It seemed at the time like the honorable thing to do, but thinking back, it was a tactical error.

I let go the death grip I had on my enemy and stepped back. He quickly climbed to his feet and slinked over to where the others were waiting.

"You can't let a mangy mutt get away with that," another coyote said. "We've got a reputation in this forest. If word gets out that we backed down from a fight with a *dog*, we won't be about to hold our heads up around here."

"You know, you're absolutely right," the defeated coyote said. He was grinning. "What was I thinking?" He turned in my direction. "Hey, tough guy, you should have finished me off when you had the chance. Because now it *is* three against one." He licked his chops, smiled at the others, and nodded. The second offensive was about to begin.

The courage I had experienced a moment earlier was now replaced by survival instinct. It was time to go—and fast. I turned on my heels and fled as quickly as three good limbs and one bum leg could carry me.

I streaked through the forest faster than I had ever moved in my life. I only wished old Mr. Davis were still alive to see me now. He would surely have convinced some family to take me home with them.

I had no idea in what direction I was headed, and I guessed it really didn't matter. Anywhere safe would be fine with me.

As I sprinted past trees, bushes, fallen branches, hollow logs—you name it—I was hoping my hunters would eventually get tired and settle for some other easier prey along the way, although I didn't wish harm on anyone. I just wanted to come out of this in one piece.

I had been moving at breakneck speed for several minutes when I stopped to catch my breath. I wasn't sure if I could afford to take a break, but I needed to rest. I scanned the area—no one in sight. The only sounds came from crickets and owls—the typical chatter one might expect to hear in the woods at night. Had I successfully shaken my pursuers? Was I actually safe now?

I wasn't quite sure. I slipped in behind a rotted-out tree that looked like it had been hit by lightning. I decided to stay right there until either the coyotes reappeared or I was certain I was safe.

Minutes later, it was clear the chase was far from over.

"We got you surrounded, pal," the lead coyote called out. "It's over."

I peeked out from behind the tree. He was standing in the clearing about thirty feet in front of me. To my left stood another member of his crew, and to my right, the third coyote. The only open direction was behind me. I had no idea where it led, but that was the least of my problems. I didn't wait around for small talk. I turned and ran.

"Get him," one of the coyotes howled.

I hoped and prayed I would somehow outrun them. I knew that if I ran in a straight line, they would eventually overtake me, so I began to zigzag in an attempt to confuse them. It seemed to be working, but they were still gaining on me.

In the distance I could see what looked like lights. Was it a house or some other kind of building? Then I realized the lights were moving. They were headlights from cars

—speeding cars. I was on a path that would lead me right onto the interstate.

I pulled up and looked around. I needed to head in another direction, but that was now impossible. I was trapped. The coyotes had managed to cut off every escape route.

I was faced with another decision. Should I risk crossing the highway? I knew it was dangerous. My mother had told me stories of dogs who had wandered off the farm, never to be seen again. They had made the mistake of trying to cross a busy highway at night. What were my chances? I wondered.

Still, I needed to make a choice—tangle with the coyotes, which was certain death, or try to cross the interstate, which I *probably* would never survive.

The coyotes stopped in their tracks. They knew the danger ahead, and they were smart enough to avoid a busy highway. If I were to somehow get across, I knew I'd be free. They'd never follow me. It was literally do or die.

I stood there trying to build up the nerve to do something—anything. A moment later, the decision had been made for me. The coyotes seemed to signal one another and then, in a mad rush, sprinted right at me.

I took a deep breath, turned, and ran in the direction of the interstate. I put my head down and awaited the inevitable. When I could feel the hard surface under my front paws, I knew I had reached the shoulder of the road. *This will be over soon—one way or another*, I thought.

The last thing I remember was the blaring sound of a horn and a blinding light. After that, there was total darkness.

When I finally woke up, I felt as though I were floating in space. I couldn't feel my body. My eyes were still closed. I was afraid to open them. I wondered if I was in heaven. My mother had talked about a place like that. I was anxious to see what it looked like.

I opened my eyes just enough to see out. What I saw was anything but heaven. The three coyotes were hovering over me.

"He looks dead," one of them said.

"What'd you expect? Who'd be dumb enough to run across a road like that?" another one said.

"So, are we gonna have an early breakfast right here or take him back to the den?" the third one said.

I closed my eyes. Right then, I was wishing that I *was* dead. That way, whatever they had planned for me would be painless.

"I'm kind of hungry," the lead coyote said, "and I don't much feel like dragging him back…unless you guys want to?"

The others shook their heads.

"Okay, then, let's have at it."

I couldn't believe what a mess I had gotten myself into. It didn't get much worse than this. I was only hoping my mother would never find out what had actually happened to me. It would break her heart.

Then I heard footsteps. They were quiet at first. Then they started to get louder. Someone was running toward us.

"Get outta there," someone shouted. "Get away from him."

The coyotes started growling. They weren't about to surrender their meal. I opened my eyes to see what was happening.

A human was running toward us. He wasn't very old —a teenager, maybe. He was carrying a baseball bat.

The coyotes surrounded me. They were ready for a showdown.

"I'll use this if I have to," the teen said, holding up the bat. He approached cautiously. "I'm not bluffing." He moved a few steps forward, then raised the bat over his head. "You asked for it."

The coyotes, apparently realizing he meant business, began to back away slowly. They continued snarling.

The teen swung the bat wildly. The coyotes immediately scattered. The kid never actually came close to making contact, but he certainly made his point.

A minute earlier, I'd thought I was a goner. Now, my hunters were nowhere in sight. I looked up at the person who had saved my life. Was he going to take me home with him? I wondered. That would be incredible. This tragedy could actually have a happy ending.

He knelt next to me, scooped me up, and carried me back to his…Oh, no, another pickup truck. The last time I had ridden in one, my life had completely changed, and not for the better. I could only hope things would be different this time.

The boy gently set me down in the bed of the pickup, closed the back gate, and sighed.

"I don't know what to do with you. But I can't just leave you out here…with *them*," he said. He sighed. "I'm not even supposed to be out here right now. It's way past my curfew. My parents are gonna to kill me." He seemed to think for a moment, then hopped in the cab and started the engine. He leaned his head out the window. "Hold on back there."

I didn't know what to think. Where were we headed? I was starting to get some feeling back in my body. My back legs hurt a lot. I wasn't sure how badly I was hurt.

As we pulled onto the road, I tried to stand. I managed to get my front half up, but my rear legs just wouldn't cooperate. I lay back down.

I knew the truck had hit me pretty hard and had messed me up some, but I was just happy to be alive. I began to wonder if this kid was destined to become my new owner. I'd be okay with that. He seemed like a good guy—a brave guy, even. Not everybody would have saved me from those coyotes. This might just work out great.

I was starting to get cold, but that was okay. I wasn't complaining. Anything was better than being somebody's main course back in the forest.

I looked around the back of the truck. There were some old paint cans, a few rags, and what looked like a blanket. I tried to relax. A little while later, I made out streetlights up ahead.

The truck slowed down and eventually came to a stop in front of a redbrick building. The sign on the front read STONYBROOK ANIMAL HOSPITAL.

So, that's it. He's gonna get me fixed up. This was one stand-up guy.

He stepped out of the truck cab, came around to the back, and opened the tailgate.

"I'm afraid this is where you get off," he said.

He reached in, pulled me over, lifted me up, and carried me to the front door. He set me down carefully on the porch.

"I'm sorry about all this, pal," he said. "You shouldn't have run out in front of me like that. I didn't want to hit you."

47

I raised my head and barked weakly.

"Don't be mad at me," he said. "I gotta get home. I'm in enough trouble as it is."

I wasn't mad at him. Why do all humans think that every time we bark, we're upset about something? I wasn't upset. I was just trying to say thanks, and hoping maybe he'd stick around a little longer and keep me company.

"Listen, they're gonna take real good care of you here. In the morning, when Doc Michaels gets in, he'll fix you up like new. You wait and see."

I put my head down. It appeared that I wasn't about to get a new owner after all. Oh, well.

The teen ran back to the truck and seemed to be fumbling for something in the back. I was shivering as I watched him. He reappeared with a blanket. He wrapped it around me. It felt so good.

"Bye, pal," he said. "Good luck."

I watched as my rescuer jogged back to his truck and disappeared into the night. I wanted to sleep, but I was afraid to close my eyes. I had been the victim of so many bad things in the past few hours I was afraid some other disaster might happen if I allowed myself to drift off.

I fought the urge to sleep for a long time but eventually lost the battle. The last thing I remember was staring at a pair of skunks on the front lawn who were searching for food. After that, I don't recall a thing.

Chapter 5

Saved by the Bell

When I opened my eyes, I realized I wasn't cold anymore. And I wasn't outside, either. I was lying on some sort of table that was covered with white paper.

I glanced upward and quickly looked away. The light hanging above me was so bright I couldn't look at it for more than a second. But there was an upside—the light was nice and warm.

Then I noticed a man leaning over looking at me. He wore a name tag on the front of his white coat. It read *Jay Michaels, DVM*. He tried to stretch out my back legs. It really hurt when he did that.

On the other side of the table was a woman wearing a light-blue jacket. I couldn't quite make out her name.

"What do you think?" she said to the doctor.

"I don't think we have a choice. We're going to have to put him down."

"What a shame," the woman said.

Put me down where? What was he talking about?

"There isn't anything you can do?" she asked as she stroked my head.

"Both back legs are broken—one of them in three places. If he were someone's pet, we could try to set them, but since he appears to be just a stray, I think we only have one option."

"So, should we prepare for surgery, then?" the woman said hopefully.

Dr. Michaels straightened up and sighed.

"Karen, who do you think is going to pay for that? We can't operate on every animal someone dumps on our front porch. We'd go broke."

"But he's such a beautiful dog," she said. "It's a real shame."

Just then, a bell rang in another room.

"Would you see who's out there?" the doctor said.

Karen nodded and left. The doc reached up and turned off the big light overhead. He patted the top of my head.

"I'm sorry, buddy. I wish there was some other way."

I lifted my head and looked him square in the eye. I didn't know what was going on, exactly, but it sure didn't sound good.

"I'm doing you a favor," he said. "I'm going to make that hurt go away."

I heard voices coming from the hallway. A woman walked in holding one end of a leash. On the other end was a bulldog who was whimpering. There appeared to be blood on his lips.

The doctor shook his head. "What did Jaws do this time?" he asked.

"Same as before," she said. "He chewed right through a metal cage."

The doctor crouched down and inspected the bulldog's mouth.

"I don't think he'll need any stitches, Vickie. Looks like he's going to need a stronger prescription, though."

"He's got the worst case of separation anxiety I've ever seen," Vickie said. She scratched Jaws behind his ear and then pointed at me. "Is that him, Karen?"

Karen, who had followed Jaws and his owner into the surgery, nodded.

Vickie came over to the examining table, lifted my head, and kissed me right on the end of my snout.

"What a sweetheart." She turned to the doctor. "You can't put him down, Doc. You just can't."

"What choice do I have, Vickie?" he said. "He's gonna need some costly surgery just to put him back together, and I don't think your rescue group has the resources to pay for it."

"We don't call ourselves a no-kill shelter for nothing," Vickie told him. "If we didn't do everything in our power to save him, then we wouldn't be doing our job."

Doc Michaels forced a smile. "And after all that expense, who do you suppose is going to adopt a dog like this? He's bound to have a noticeable limp for the rest of his life."

"You'd be surprised," she said. "There are people out there who might really be drawn to him."

"Oh, really?" he said skeptically.

"Even if no one ever adopted him, and he had to stay with us, he'd at least have a chance at life."

And so the second chapter of my young life began.

Doc Michaels fixed me up the best he could. I wasn't looking for miracles—just, as Vickie put it, *a chance at life*.

I certainly wasn't worried about some silly limp. I'd lived with one my entire life.

When I came out of surgery, both of my back legs were in casts. I didn't know how this sort of thing worked. Would these become my new legs? Would they stay on permanently? I tried standing up, but it was just too uncomfortable.

I had to admit I was starting to get pretty bummed out. I couldn't imagine living the rest of my life like this. Before, I had a bad leg, but I could at least still get around. This was completely different. I couldn't imagine always needing somebody to take me from Point A to Point B. And who would that person be? Who would ever adopt me in this condition? Who would ever want a freak like me?

Every time I looked at my new legs, I knew I would never become someone's watchdog. I had always believed that, even though it might have been a long shot, it wasn't impossible for a basset hound with a game leg to become a watchdog. But there was just no way folks looking to protect their home and family would ever adopt a dog like me.

And that was only the half of it. Even if I scared away people who wanted a watchdog, I very much doubted even someone just looking for your run-of the-mill house pet would bother to take a chance on me. People wanted a pet they could run with, and romp with, and play with, and that wasn't me.

I stayed with Doc Michaels for a few days before Vickie came to pick me up. She took me to my new home—The Bardmoor Rescue Center. This place was nothing like the breeding farm. Instead of basset hounds everywhere, there was every kind of dog and cat imaginable. And they all seemed pretty vocal about having a new boarder. I got a lot of stares when Vickie carried me in and placed me in my own cage.

She seemed awfully nice, but I wasn't sure what I had done wrong. Was she mad at me or something? I mean, why else would she have locked me up? In fact, all of the dogs in my section were locked up. Were they all criminals? Most of them didn't look mean or anything.

To be honest, I was confused. Why, exactly, would you rescue a dog if you were just going to put him in jail? It didn't make any sense.

When the barking finally died down, a black Scottish terrier in the cage to my left poked his head out from under a towel and stared at me.

"Hi," I said. "My name's Rutherford. What's yours?"

The Scottie disappeared under the towel.

"I won't hurt you," I said. "I'm a pretty friendly guy." I could see the little dog was shaking. I wasn't sure what to say to make him relax and trust me. "So, tell me something. Why are all you guys in cages? What'd you do that was so bad?"

The Scottie popped his head out. "What are you talking about? We didn't do anything bad."

"Then why are you locked up?" I asked.

"It isn't 'cause we did anything wrong. It's just how it is here." He came out from under the towel and over to my side of his cage.

"What kind of a place is this, anyway?" I said.

"It's a shelter," he said. "It's a place where people come to adopt dogs and cats and take them home."

Take them home? Did I hear him right? "You mean, to be family pets?"

"Well, sure, silly. Why else would somebody adopt us?"

I couldn't believe what I was hearing. This was sensational news. Maybe I did have a chance of going home with a real family after all.

"Well, that still doesn't explain why we're all in cages." I said.

The Scottie shook his head. "Can you imagine what this place would be like if we were all loose and running around? It'd be chaos, I tell you. I, for one, am delighted to be in this cage. It just makes a body feel a lot safer.

"And I don't think the people who come by to adopt us would feel too comfortable if we were running all over the place. Face it—it just works better this way. And most of us are only here a few weeks before we're adopted anyway."

A few weeks? That was nothing. I could handle that.

"So, how long have you been here?" I asked.

"Tell him, Boomer," a voice said from the cage on the other side of mine. "Tell him you've been here for nearly two years."

The Scottie, whose name was apparently Boomer, slipped back underneath his towel. I wiggled around to discover a collie. She had gray hair on her forehead and snout. She looked like an old-timer.

"Welcome, friend," she said. "My name's Marge. Happy to make your acquaintance."

"Hi," I said. "I'm Rutherford. I just got here."

"I can see that," she said. "What's your story?"

Boomer came out from under his towel and placed his nose up against the side of the cage to listen.

"Well, I was born on a breeding farm a few miles from here. It's for basset hounds. You know—the kind of place where people come if they're looking for a show dog. I've been living there with my mom and my brothers and sisters for a couple of years—"

"Whoa! Whoa!" Marge barked. "The condensed version, please."

"Oh, sorry."

Boomer smiled at me. "You don't have to rush for me," he said. "I've got all day."

"Speak for yourself," Marge said. "I'm twelve years old. I want to be alive when he finishes."

At this point, I don't mind telling you, I was a little confused. If this shelter place was where you lived for a few weeks while you waited to be adopted, then why had Boomer been here for almost two years, and why was an old dog like Marge still around?

"So, if you don't mind my asking," I said, "why have you two been here so long?"

Boomer dropped his head. He seemed embarrassed.

"For a little guy, Boomer's had a rough go of it," Marge said. "He got adopted about a year ago, and let's just say his owner wasn't very nice to him. On top of that, he just dumped him one day."

"I know what that's like," I said.

"Did you get thrown out of a car going seventy miles an hour?" she said.

I glanced at Boomer. He was still staring at the floor. I had been feeling sorry for myself, but now I felt a little guilty.

"People make me a little nervous now," Boomer said.

"A little?" Marge said.

"Well, a lot, I guess," he replied.

When I glanced at him, he immediately looked away. It seemed like he was nervous around everyone, including other dogs.

"So, whenever someone walks by his cage, Boomer hides under his towel," Marge said. "No offense, Boomer, but no one's interested in a pet who's afraid of everything."

"I know," he said dejectedly.

I turned to Marge. "And what about you?"

"Oh, my story is completely different," she said. "I lived with the same family my entire life—husband and wife lawyers. They never had any kids—just me. But about six months ago, the mister fell and broke his hip. So, they sold their house and moved in with their daughter —who just happens to be allergic to dogs. So, here I am. It's okay, though. I don't mind. I really enjoyed my time with them. And, hey, if you ever need any legal advice, you just ask. I learned a lot from my owners."

"You've been here how long? Six months?" I asked.

"And I'll probably be here a lot longer," she said. "Let's face it—nobody wants a twelve-year-old dog. I've accepted the fact I'll be here for the rest of my natural days."

I decided I liked Marge. She seemed so wise. She reminded me of my mother.

"But I'm perfectly fine with it," she said. "They treat us pretty good here. And as long as Boomer's around to keep me company, I'm perfectly content."

The sound of snoring caught our attention.

"What was that noise?" I said.

Marge pointed to the cage on the other side of Boomer's, where a bulldog was fast asleep. He looked vaguely familiar.

"Who's that?" I asked.

"Oh, that's Jaws," she said.

Of course, now I remembered. He was the dog Vickie brought into the vet the day we'd met.

"Poor old Jaws," Marge said. "He suffers from separation anxiety."

"What's that?"

"Whenever he's left alone," Boomer said, "he freaks out. He starts chewing stuff—blankets, blinds, carpeting, clothes, you name it."

Marge chuckled. "And what a set of choppers. I swear he could gnaw his way through solid steel. He's already chewed through two of the cages."

"He looks kind of scary," I said.

"Jaws? No way. He's a sweetheart," Marge said. "He'll make a great pet for someone. But, because of the chewing, he'll probably be here for a long time, just like me and Boomer.

"I'm sure you'll get adopted right away, Rutherford," Boomer said.

"You really think someone's going to adopt me like this. I can't even walk right. Look at these things." I tried to stand up but it really hurt.

"So, what's the big deal?" Boomer said. "Those casts will come off in a couple of months, and you'll be good as new."

"What?" I said. "You mean these things come off?"

Marge started laughing. "What did you think, silly? That those casts were permanent?"

"I can't tell you how many dogs with broken legs have been brought in here," Boomer said. "And weeks later, they're running around the place."

I couldn't believe it. Once I healed up, I might actually get adopted. But what condition would my legs be in once the casts came off? I might even have a worse limp than I did before.

"So, how did you end up here?" Marge asked again.

"It's a long story," I said. Marge's eyes narrowed. "But here's the condensed version."

She smiled.

"Since I wasn't what you'd call show-dog material, the breeder dumped me in the woods. Then I had a little altercation with a pack of coyotes. And when I tried to get away from them, I ran onto the interstate—and the rest is history."

Marge reached her right front paw through an opening in the cage and began stroking my forehead.

"I'm sorry about all of that," she said, "But I'm glad you're here with us.'

"Me, too," Boomer said.

A door opened at the end of the aisle, and someone came in. The other residents immediately began barking. It was Vickie. She walked up to my cage, bent down, and unlocked the door.

"I've got a surprise for you," she said. "We've been working on it all morning." She crouched down and placed her hands on the front of Boomer's and Marge's cages.

They began licking her.

"Wait until you two see what we have planned for your new friend here," she said.

And what she had planned would turn out to be utterly amazing.

Chapter 6
Wheels of Fortune

Vickie carried me out through the kennel and down a long hallway. The other boarders continued to be fairly vocal as we passed their cages. We eventually stopped at a door marked *Pet Infirmary*. Vickie pushed it open with her hip, then set me down on a soft table. It almost felt like a leather couch. Very comfy.

The room reminded me of the one where Doc Michaels had fixed me up. It kind of smelled like it, too. The walls were filled with shelves, and on each one were dozens of tiny bottles.

"What are you looking at?" Vickie said. "Don't worry. Nothing bad's gonna happen."

She reached under the table and brought out what had to be the strangest-looking contraption I had ever seen. It was about a foot and a half long, and looked like a little chariot. The only difference was that the front of it was open. It had straps coming out from the bottom that appeared to be little belts. And there were two rubber wheels in the back.

"Confused?" Vickie said.

Of course I was confused. What was this thing? And what did it have to do with me?

She set it down on the table next to me.

"All ready for your new set of legs?" she asked.

She lifted me up, and set the back half of my body into this little chariot. Then she grabbed the belts and strapped me in.

I wasn't quite sure if I liked this or not, but I was willing to give her the benefit of the doubt. After all, if it hadn't been for Vickie, I'd be in Doggie Heaven right now.

"What do you say?" she said, "Let's test it out."

She lifted me up, chariot and all, and set me down onto the floor. She then walked across the room, turned and faced me. She dug her hand into her pocket and pulled out a handful of treats. She now had my complete attention. She crouched down and held out her hand, palm up, full of goodies.

"Okay, boy, come and get it."

I ran in her direction. I didn't even stop to think that I was now towing some strange device. I made it over to where Vickie was standing in record time and lapped up the treats. Mmm, liver, my favorite.

She stood up and clapped her hands. "It works! It works!" she said. She reached down and stroked my head. "So, what do you think? You're complete again. A brand new set of legs until your old ones heal up."

What was she talking about? I was still savoring those tasty morsels. I hadn't realized what was going on. I glanced over my shoulder and stared at the little chariot. It was still connected to me. I had dragged it all the way across the room, but it had been effortless. I didn't even know I had done it.

I thought about what she had just said: "a brand new set of legs." Wait a minute. Of course. Those wheels were my new temporary legs.

I had heard about this kind of gadget somewhere. It must have been from my mother. I remembered her telling me about a friend of hers who had gotten into an accident with a piece of farm machinery one time, and who had gotten new legs just like these.

That situation had been much worse. Her friend had lost all use of the back end of her body. She had no feeling in her hind legs, so she would have to use a cart like this for her entire life. I, luckily, would only need it for a few weeks.

I decided to test this thing out. I began walking slowly. Then I picked up my pace just a little. Then faster. This was amazing.

It was now time for the ultimate test. I ran around the table—once, twice, three times. Vickie started laughing. I just kept going. I couldn't stop myself. Not only was I flying around the room, but I think I was running faster than I had before the accident. And on top of it, had finally gotten rid of that nagging limp, at least for the time being.

I couldn't believe it. I started wagging my tail. I had to tell Vickie how happy I was. I needed to thank her.

I ran over and tried to jump up onto her. Whoa! When I put my front paws on her leg, the wheels on the cart began turning and I almost fell over backwards. Not a good move. That wasn't going to work, and I wasn't sure how else to show my appreciation.

But she sensed it. She crouched down, hugged me, and kissed me on the nose. She knew I was ecstatic, and she seemed just as happy.

"Now, there's one last thing we have to do," she said. "We have to give you a name."

But I already have a name, I thought.

Oh, well, I'd just need to make the best of it. Vickie didn't know my real name, and there was no way of telling her what it was. I had heard about things like this—where you have a name, but your new owners want to give you a new one they like better. I was just hoping it wouldn't be something embarrassing. I had an image to maintain.

"Let's see," she said. She placed her finger on her lips, thinking. A moment later, she smiled. "Yes, that's it. I don't suppose you've seen the famous chariot race in the movie *Ben-Hur*, have you?"

Movie? I had heard about them, but I had never seen any. My mother used to talk about movies like *Lassie Come-Home, 101 Dalmatians, The Shaggy Dog, Air Bud, Beethoven,* and *Scooby-Doo*. She'd told me that maybe when a family took me home some day, I might be lucky enough to see one of these movies on their TV. I didn't recall her saying anything about a movie called *Ben-Hur*.

"Well, anyway, Ben-Hur was a master of the chariot, just like you'll be soon. So, how about if we call you *Ben-Hur*?"

The expression on my face must have told her I wasn't a big fan of her choice of names.

"Okay, let's just make it *Ben*. What do you think?" she said.

©brad a. foster. 2020

It was at least short and easy to remember. I could handle that. My canine friends knew me as Rutherford, but I guess I could put up with a few humans referring to me as "Ben". Since it was Vickie who renamed me, I was fine with it. I responded by licking her hands.

"Oh, good," she said. "I'm glad you approve." She walked over to the door and opened it. "Come on, let's go show off the new you."

I followed her out of the pet infirmary, down the hall, and up to the door leading back to the kennel. With my new wheels, I had no problem keeping up. Before opening the door, Vickie held up her hand. I think she wanted me to stop. She opened the door and stepped in. The crowd immediately greeted her with a rousing round of excited barking. So, what else was new?

"Hey, guys," she said. "Can you keep it down for a minute?" She waited for the noise to die down. "Thanks. Okay, now, I have a little announcement to make." She turned back toward me and winked. Then in an official manner: "The Bardmoor Rescue Center is proud to present its newest resident. I'd like you to meet…Ben!" She opened the door all the way and motioned for me to enter.

I held my head high and pranced proudly into the kennel. As expected, the barking resumed. But it wasn't scared or angry or hungry barking; the other boarders were cheering for me in the only way they knew how. It felt great.

I marched up to my cage, waited for Vickie to swing open the door, and entered. She bent down, closed the door, and gave me a big smile.

"I'll be back in a little while to take that off. In the meantime, you can show it off to your friends."

She got up and headed for the exit. Before she reached the door, she turned back to address the troops.

"Dinner in an hour, gang," she said, and promptly disappeared.

I was so excited about my new gadget, I could hardly contain myself. I noticed Marge smiling at me.

"I can't begin to tell you how happy I am for you, Rutherford," she said. "It's like you're a new man...er, dog, that is. Just look at you."

Boomer seemed more curious than anything else.

"So, does that thing hurt or what?" he said.

"Hurt? No, not at all," I said. "To be perfectly honest, with the casts and everything, I can barely feel it. It's all good back there." I was so happy about the new me I wanted to celebrate. I wanted to throw a party. Heck, I wanted to put on a show.

Wait a minute. Of course, that was it! I *could* put on a show—a comedy routine for all of my new friends. I was fairly confident they'd love it, but maybe I should bounce a joke or two off of them just to make sure.

I found myself getting a little nervous about performing in front of an audience again, but the excitement of being able to move around seemed to give me the necessary courage to continue.

"Hey, everyone, could I have your attention, please?" I shouted.

The others looked at me quizzically. They apparently hadn't expected the new kid to speak up. But I'm a showman, and this was a way of life for me.

"I have this friend who's a Chihuahua. And this little guy just loves to dance. The problem is...he's a terrible dancer. Whenever I put on Latin music, he jumps up and starts doing the tango. Let me tell you…it's not pretty. But what do you expect? He does have four left feet."

For a moment, it was deathly quiet. Then, as if someone had suddenly turned on an applause sign, the entire room erupted with laughter and cheers.

"Hey, new guy," a greyhound yelled from across the room, "that was pretty good."

"Didn't you hear Vickie?" a poodle added, "His name is Ben."

"Okay, sorry," the greyhound said. "So, *Ben*, you got another one like that?"

Before I could respond, Marge chimed in. "His name is actually Rutherford."

"Rutherford…Ben…whatever," the greyhound said. "You got any more jokes?"

During my short lifetime, there is one thing I have learned—being able to tell a good joke is both a curse and a blessing. It's a real high when the audience laughs, but if they like you too much, they're never satisfied with just one funny story. They'll want another and another and another. I hadn't really anticipated doing an entire routine right here and now. I guess I should have.

"Well…um…let me think for a minute," I said, buying time.

When I glanced at my audience, I could see at least twenty sets of eyes, all focused on me. I thought for what seemed like an eternity. I needed something…even a marginal joke.

But to be honest, I needed a break. All that running around had taken a toll. My back legs were aching. I didn't feel much like entertaining the troops. I just wanted to rest, but I could tell the crowd was getting restless.

I was just about to apologize for coming up dry and needing to lie down when an old joke popped into my head. *Yeah, I think I can tell one more.*

"Let me tell you about this friend of mine—Bernie the golden retriever. Great guy, but whenever we're riding together, he gets carsick. It's not pleasant, let me tell you. So, we called the vet to see what he would suggest, and he came up with the perfect remedy. You know what I give Bernie now before he jumps into the car?" I paused. "Bus fare."

Like before, there were a few seconds of silence followed by hearty laughter. I guess it took the average dog a little longer to figure out the punchline. But that was okay —as long as they eventually got it.

"Tell me about it," Boomer said. "I throw up in the car all the time."

"Encore! Encore!" a beagle howled. "You're on a roll, Rutherford."

And that was exactly what I was afraid of. I leaned over in the direction of Marge's cage and whispered.

"I'm getting pretty sore. I'd just like to take it easy for a while. Can you help me out here?"

Marge smiled. "Let me handle this," she said. She stood up and cleared her throat. "Listen, everyone, Rutherford needs a little time to himself. When he got fitted with those wheels, it took a lot out of him. So, let's just respect his privacy and allow him to recuperate. Okay?"

"Okay, I guess," the greyhound said. "But we sure would like to hear more of his funny stories after he's had time to rest."

"We'll work on that," Marge said.

The other dogs returned to what they were doing. Whew! It was sure nice to have the pressure off for a little while. I guess that since Marge had been here so long, she was kind of the boss. I owed her big-time.

"Aren't we just full of surprises?" she said, settling down next to our shared wall.

"Huh?"

"Those jokes of yours," she said. "I never saw that coming."

I smiled. "Well, it's what I do. You see, when I finally accepted the fact that it might take some time for me to become a watchdog, I decided I needed another talent. Since I've always gotten a pretty good response to my jokes, I figured I'd be a comedian."

"So, you're, like, a real stand-up comic, huh?" Boomer said. "I've never known a dog who could do that. It's kind of neat. When humans tell dog jokes, they make us sound kind of stupid. But when you do it, it's just funny."

"I'll take that as a compliment," I said.

"Well, you're really going to liven up this place," Marge said. "I'm so glad Vickie found you. I think we're all going to get along just great."

You sure wouldn't get an argument from me. Living in a shelter with a pair of wheels for legs wasn't exactly the way I had envisioned my life, but things certainly could have been a lot worse. I was surrounded by friends, human and canine, who seemed to enjoy having me around. Maybe I was finally home.

Chapter 7

Command Performance

The days that passed next were glorious. I got a chance to meet most of the other boarders. All of them had nice things to say about my stand-up routine. And they all asked when the next performance would take place. I kept telling them I was working on some new material, and that I needed a little more time to clean up a few rough spots. Everybody was pretty patient, but I knew I would eventually have to set an official date for my next show.

When I wasn't writing jokes or chatting with friends, I would spend my time watching families stop by to look us over. On average, a couple of us would be adopted each week. I always had mixed feelings when Vickie would come in and announce who was leaving us. We would all cheer and wish them well but you could kind of tell that most of us were envious. It's not that we were unhappy living at the shelter; it was just that we all selfishly wanted a chance to make it on the outside.

Marge, Boomer, and I were realists. We never expected to leave this place, and we were okay with that. As long as we three stayed together, we were just fine. Every once in a while, a visitor would pay special attention to one of us. It was both exciting and nerve-wracking at the same time. As much as we wanted to get adopted, we knew we'd feel really guilty about leaving the other two behind.

We soon realized we had nothing to worry about. Once people got a good look, it didn't take them long to eliminate us from their search. I would have been perfectly fine if they had just moved on and said nothing, but many would make comments about us. I knew they weren't trying to hurt our feelings, that it was just that they didn't know we could understand them.

"Look at that one," they'd say about Boomer. "He's cute, but there's just something not right about him." It didn't help, of course, that Boomer spent most of his time under a towel whenever people came by. Sometimes they'd think he was playing, but they'd soon realize he was afraid of… well…everything. And no one wanted to take on a project. They wanted things nice and easy. What they didn't realize was that, with the proper amount of love and affection, Boomer would have made a great pet.

The comments about Marge were predictable. "Look at how old that dog is," they'd say. "Who'd want to adopt a dog who might die in three or four years?" It was pretty cruel. You don't have to remind us how short our lives are. We're painfully aware of it. But did people have to say those things right in front of us? And loud enough for us to hear? It was downright rude.

Other dogs wouldn't have handled those comments very well but Marge was a real trouper. She knew she wasn't going anywhere, but she never complained.

"I feel sorry for people like that," she would say. "There's a lot to be said for older dogs. We're stable, we're loyal, and we're not selfish like puppies."

Amen. I couldn't have agreed more

One nice thing about the shelter was that you rarely had to deal with puppies. I guess you've figured out by now that I have this thing about them. I'm not proud of it, but I can't help myself. I get so tired of them getting all the attention. People seem to forget that they chew up the furniture, they cry all night, and have absolutely no bladder control. It's amazing what folks will put up with just because puppies are so darn cute.

Why can't folks realize that a more mature animal is an even better pet? Sure, we're not as cute, but cute lasts just so long. When it's worn off, those same people bring their puppies right back to the shelter, and they end up adopting an older pet. Duh! I could have told them that was going to happen if they'd just asked me.

If they had, I know just what I'd tell them. I'd say that mature dogs are more worldly. They have more street smarts. They're house-trained, for Pete's sake. And don't get me started about protection. If you're out walking a puppy, and you happen to come across a feisty raccoon, don't expect any help from the pup. They just turn tail and run. But an older dog will put up a fight to the finish to protect his owner.

Oh, there I go again--getting all worked up about it. I'd just better let it go.

One day, after having been pestered incessantly by the other boarders, I announced my next performance. It would take place on the upcoming Saturday night right after feeding time. In preparation for the big event, I began mentally jotting down and memorizing any joke I thought they might like. This audience would expect killer material. My original informal routine had apparently whetted their appetites for a real showstopper.

When the big day arrived, I was ready, or at least I thought I was. After Vickie took her final walkthrough of the kennel to make sure we all had eaten, the curtain was about to rise. Marge had offered to do the introduction. Boomer flipped his metal food dish upside down and began pounding on it as if it were a snare drum.

"Ladies and gentlemen," Marge announced, "Can we have your attention, please. First of all, let me remind you that flash photography is strictly forbidden. And please silence all cell phones and electronic devices." She paused for a moment and grinned. She seemed to be enjoying herself.

She turned to Boomer and nodded. It was his cue to begin the official drum roll.

"The Bardmoor Rescue Center is proud to present a sensational new performer who recently finished an engagement at the Davis Breeding Farm. So, if you're quite ready, please give it up for Rutherford, Canine Comic."

Barking, howling, and other similar sounds followed. I rolled up to the front of the cage, took a deep breath, and smiled nervously. Ready or not, this was it.

"Thanks so much, folks. It's great to be here," I said.

Marge nodded approvingly, while Boomer sported an ear-to-ear grin. He would be my wingman. It was so great to have the support of friends.

"Hey, did you hear about the businessman who was looking for some office help?" I said. "He hung a sign in his front window that read: *Help Wanted. Must be able to type. Must be good with computers. Must be bilingual. We are an equal-opportunity employer.*

"So, a little later, this dog strolls up, reads the sign, and goes in. He walks up to the receptionist and wags his tail. Then he points to the sign in the window and barks. Sensing that the dog wanted to apply for the job, the receptionist goes and gets her boss.

"When the boss sees the dog, he says, 'Listen, pal, I can't hire you. The sign says you have to be able to type.' With that, the dog spots an empty desk, jumps up into the chair, and begins typing. In no time, he cranks out a perfect business letter.

"He gives it to the stunned man, who says: 'Very impressive. But you also have to be good with a computer.' The dog immediately opens up a program on the computer and in no time produces a perfect spreadsheet.

"Needless to say, the boss is amazed. He looks at the dog and says, 'I have to admit—you're a really talented little fellow. But here's the problem, you also have to be bilingual.

"The dog smiles, looks the man straight in the eye, and says, 'Meow.'"

Boomer tapped a rawhide bone on his water dish and produced a timely rim shot. The kennel went mad—barking, howling, and even some playful growling.

"Rutherford, you're killing me," the greyhound said.

"You got a real talent," the beagle added.

A Dalmatian who had recently joined the group chimed in, "Yeah, that was outstanding."

I winked at Boomer. His rim shot had been perfect. He was almost as good as Daphne.

"Don't stop there," the greyhound said.

I had no intention of stopping. I waited a moment for the commotion to die down.

"So, did you hear about the dog who walks into a bar?" I said. "He goes up to the bartender and says, 'Hey, do you have any bacon?' The bartender says, 'Sorry, we don't have any.' About a half-hour later, the dog comes back in and says, 'Hey, do you have any bacon?' The bartender says, 'I already told you—we don't have any.' A few minutes later, the dog comes back in and says, 'Hey, do you have any bacon?'

"By this time, the bartender has had just about enough. He tells the dog, 'Listen, if you ask me that one more time, I'm gonna nail your paws to the floor.' About ten minutes later, the dog walks back in, goes up to the bartender and says, 'Hey, do you have any nails?'

"'No,' the bartender says.

"'In that case,' the dog says, 'do you have any bacon?'"

Rim shot.

By this time the audience was out of control—barking, whistling, hooting. A couple of the dogs laughed so hard they fell backward and knocked their water dishes over, completely soaking themselves. But it didn't bother them in the least. They were having too good a time to care.

"Hey, you guys, I hear a noise in the hallway," the greyhound said. "I think someone's coming."

A second later, Vickie walked in. "What's going on in here?" she said. "What's all the commotion?"

By that time, the kennel was perfectly quiet. We were all lying down, pretending to be fast asleep.

Vickie scratched her head. "I'm sure I heard something." She began inspecting the cages. "It's okay for you guys to make a little noise," she said. "I just wanted to be sure everything was okay." She glanced down and noticed the cart still connected to the back half of my body. She unlocked my cage and leaned in."

"I think you're done with this for the day." She undid the straps, slid it off, and placed it on top of the cage then took one last look at all of us. Once she was certain we were all fine, she turned to leave. "Goodnight, fellas and gals."

As soon as the door closed, we opened our eyes and sat up.

"Boy, that was close," Boomer said.

"Yeah, we'd better end the show right here," Marge said. She turned to me. "Rutherford, you're just too funny for your own good."

"I could listen to you all night," the beagle said. "How do you do it, anyway? How do you come up with this stuff?"

"I don't know," I said. "Funny stuff just pops into my head."

But that wasn't how it was at all. Writing jokes is really hard. Personally, I think some of the most talented writers in the world are comedy writers. Just think of it—you have to find material that *everyone* finds humorous. What a Jack Russell terrier would laugh at, I guarantee a malamute won't. You have to come up with material that speaks a universal language—something that every breed will enjoy. And that's tough.

Vickie's appearance was actually a blessing. I'd still had a few more jokes in my arsenal, so I was able to tuck them away until my next command performance. And those were beginning to happen on an almost daily basis. There was no satisfying this crowd. If they had their way, I'd be on stage every night.

But that was an impossibility—'cause there just weren't that many funny dog stories out there. One thing I was particularly proud of was the fact that I never once repeated a joke. These guys had great memories. They would have remembered a recycled effort.

And so, in the days that followed at the Bardmoor Rescue Center, I spent my time playing and chatting with Boomer and Marge and some of the other folks. When I managed to find some spare time, I would work on new material. It was a pretty good life. And if I ever started feeling sorry for myself, I would just think back to my final days on the breeding farm after Mr. Davis had died, or my near-death experience in the woods.

Ever since my little accident a few weeks back on the highway, I'd never once complained about having two bad flippers and having to pull the rear half of my body by mini-chariot. It's just who I was now, and I'd simply accepted that for the time being. I *was* anxious to get the casts off my legs, but I was also a little scared. What if my bones hadn't healed properly? What if I had to pull around the cart for the rest of my life?

I refused to think about it. I preferred thinking about the day when a family would come in looking for a real watchdog, and walk out with yours truly. And although I knew it was a long shot, I never gave up hope.

🐾 🐾 🐾

A week or so later, we noticed Vickie and the other volunteers were working long hours. They were cleaning the walls, scrubbing the floors, and hanging decorations all around. Each of the residents was treated to a bubble bath, nail-trim, and ear-cleaning. They even put bows on some of the girl dogs. When one of the staff members tried putting a bow on me, I let her know in no uncertain terms that I was a boy…all boy. It didn't take her long to get the message.

Within a couple of days, the place was all spruced up, and we were looking—and smelling—pretty good.

"What's up?" I asked Marge. "What's going on around here?"

"Oh, that's right," she said. "You're still a newbie. The volunteers do this every year for something called Adopt-a-Pet Week."

"Adopt-a-Pet Week?" I said. "What's that?"

Marge smiled and shook her head. "Don't worry, it won't affect you or me or Boomer. We aren't going anywhere. But it might change the lives of some of the others."

I scratched my forehead. "I still don't know what you're talking about."

"Every year around this time, the shelter goes all-out," she said. "They put on this big advertising thing about the plight of animals like us—ones who need permanent homes. Sometimes the local newspaper picks it up. Last year, one of the radio stations even did a story about us.

"All that publicity really helped, and it doesn't hurt that they cut the adoption fee in half. A lot of people come by, and a lot of dogs were adopted."

"Really?" I said. "Maybe this *is* our chance."

"I wouldn't put money on it," Marge said. "Everybody seems to want the perfect dog, and I'm afraid you, me, and Boomer aren't what they have in mind."

"But we'd be good pets," I said. "Heck, we'd make *great* pets."

Marge smiled. "I know that, and you know that, but just try convincing the humans." She reached through the cage and stroked the top of my head—just like my mom used to. "Do me a favor, Rutherford. Don't get your hopes up, okay? I don't want to see you disappointed."

I thought for a minute. I was torn between wanting to be adopted, and wanting to stay right here with Marge and Boomer. I knew one thing for sure—I couldn't bear the thought of either one of *them* leaving—or even worse, both of them leaving.

For the remainder of the afternoon, I found myself trying to imagine this place without them. I was starting to get really depressed. And then, all at once, I thought about what I was doing.

It was selfish of me to think like that. If Marge or Boomer got adopted, it would be so great for them. They'd make some families really happy. And if I was a true friend, I'd celebrate with them—no matter how much it hurt.

Chapter 8

End of a Career

When the doors opened the next day, marking the official start of Adopt-a-Pet Week, I wasn't ready for what happened next. A line of future pet owners had formed on the front sidewalk, and it curled all the way back to the parking lot. For the entire day—from eight in the morning to well past six at night—people paraded through the kennel.

On the first day, our friend the greyhound was snatched up. A day later, the Dalmatian went home with new owners. The day after that, the beagle was adopted. Even Jaws lucked out—a lady who worked from home decided to take a chance on him. It seemed like the perfect fit. That way he wouldn't be alone too much.

I was really happy for all our friends, but I was a little jealous, too. I wished it had been me.

By the end of the week, half of the cages were empty; but as expected, Marge, Boomer, and I were still in what was likely to be our permanent home. Marge was right—

we weren't going anywhere. That was fine with me. We were still together, and that's all that mattered. Soon the empty cages would be full again.

The week seemed to fly by. It was nearing closing time on Friday, and the crowd had thinned out to a handful of potential owners. Things would soon be back to normal.

Out of the corner of my eye, I noticed an older lady with a cane wearing a bright-red hat approaching us. Vickie was holding her by the arm. They stopped right in front of Marge's cage.

"This is the one I was telling you about," Vickie said. "Her name is Tulip." Marge rolled her eyes. It was another name the shelter had come up with. "She's older than the others, but she's calm and loving and would make a wonderful pet for someone."

"How old, exactly?" the woman said.

"Tulip was twelve on her last birthday."

I knew that once the old woman heard how old Marge was, she'd lose interest. It wasn't personal, mind you. That's just how it was.

The woman bent down the best she could and took a closer look at Marge, who had come over to greet her.

"Can we take her out so I can get to know her a little better?" the old woman said.

"Of course," Vickie said. She unlocked the cage and swung open the door. "Come on out and say hello, Tulip."

The proud collie proceeded slowly out of her cage and sat at the woman's feet. Marge started smelling her all over. That may have seemed a little rude, but this was a big decision for both of them, and it was best to know as much as possible about a potential owner.

I was just waiting for the old lady to say something like "She seems really sweet, but do you have any who aren't quite this old?" Instead, she leaned over, held Marge's head in both hands, and said, "She's perfect. We both move at about the same speed. I'll take her."

Marge looked up and smiled. She began licking the woman's hands.

The woman turned to Vickie. "It's almost as if she knew what I said."

Well, duh, of course we know what humans say. But we'll never let on.

"It does, doesn't it?" Vickie said. She grabbed a leash off a hook on the wall and attached it to Marge's collar. "Let's go into the office and do some paperwork, shall we?"

The old woman glanced at the rest of us as she followed Vickie and Marge past the other cages. Boomer, who had spent the last few minutes under his towel, stuck his head out.

"What's happening?" he said. "Where are they taking Marge?"

I was afraid to tell him the truth, but I knew he'd find out sooner or later. It was best to be honest.

"She's headed to her new home," I said.

"New home?" Boomer said. "You mean she got adopted?"

I nodded.

"It can't be. It just can't be," he said. "Marge said we'd be together forever."

I sort of knew what Boomer was feeling. Marge was like a mother to him. When Horace dumped me in the woods, I knew I'd probably never see my own mother again. It had left me with an empty feeling—one that never completely goes away. Now it looked like I would need to take Marge's place and look out for Boomer.

I was sure I could do that—even with temporary wheels for legs. After all, I had seen my mother care for dozens of puppies over the years. How difficult could it be to take care of one frightened little dog?

Boomer crawled back under his towel. "It'll never be the same around here again," he said. "I wish I was dead."

"Stop that," I said. "I don't ever want to hear you talk like that."

"How could she do that?" he said. "How could she just leave us?"

"Aren't you the least bit happy for her?"

Boomer poked his head out again.

"Well, I guess so, but…" He started to tear up. "Who's going to help me now? Marge was teaching me how to not be afraid."

"I'd be happy to help," I said.

Boomer looked hopeful. "Really? Would you?"

"Sure."

The door at the far end of the kennel suddenly opened and slammed against one of the cages. A large, mean-looking man filled the doorway. Vickie was right behind him.

"Sir, I'm afraid we're about to close up for the evening," she said.

"I only need a minute," the man said. "I know exactly what I'm looking for." He marched into the kennel and glanced briefly into each cage. The expression on his face suggested he was all business. "This is *it*?" he said. "This is all you got?"

"Well, every couple of days we get in some new dogs. But this is it for the time being. You see, this is the last day of Adopt-a-Pet Week, so we're a little thin right now."

He made a face. "I don't see anything I want." He turned to leave but stopped short and did a double-take right in front of Boomer's cage. "Hey, is there something under there?"

Boomer, as usual, was completely hidden by his towel.

"Oh, that's Einstein," Vickie said. *Einstein? Who came up with that name?* I liked Boomer, but he was no Einstein. "We're still working with him. He's a little shy. Well, actually, he's *a lot* shy. I'm not sure he's ready to be adopted yet."

I couldn't put my finger…er, my paw on it, but there was something about this guy I didn't like. He seemed nothing like the other people who had come in looking for a pet.

"Can I see him?" the man said. "I love working with shy, timid dogs. I've made it my life's work. I go around to kennels and look for dogs just like your Einstein. I give them a lot of TLC, and in no time, they're full of confidence. I see a great pet in that cage just waiting for someone to show him the love and guidance that will completely turn him around.

"That sounds wonderful," Vickie said. She bent down, unlocked Boomer's cage, and tried to coax him out.

"Come on, Einstein," she said. "There's someone here I want you to meet."

As was his nature, Boomer was uncooperative. He refused to leave the towel. Vickie eventually had to reach in and slide him out. She sat down on the floor and cradled him in her lap.

There was still something about this guy that bothered me. He was saying all the right things to Vickie, but he just gave me the creeps.

"It's okay, little guy," she said. "Just relax. Nobody's going to hurt you." She looked up at the man, who hovered over her with his arms folded. "You're sure about this dog? Under normal circumstances, we wouldn't send him home with anyone. But if your methods seem to work, I guess we can let you have him

"Fantastic," the man said. "He's just what I'm looking for. How long's it gonna take to get this done?"

And just like that, the two most important living creatures in my new life were gone

I couldn't believe it. I could understand the older lady who was looking for a companion. Marge seemed to be in good hands. But why in the world did someone like that guy want Boomer? I couldn't help but think he was pulling the wool over everyone's eyes.

Don't get me wrong, Boomer was my friend—but he was a project. It would take months, maybe years, for him to trust people again. Even though he'd said otherwise, his new owner didn't look like the kind of person who would have the patience to work with a dog who needed a whole lot of love.

The days that followed were bleak. There weren't any other dogs like me—ones who expected to make this shelter their permanent home. Most would come in, get cleaned up, see a vet, and in a few days, would go off to a loving home. I got lonely.

Still, there was one good thing about the high turnover. None of the new dogs had heard my stand-up routine, so there wasn't much pressure on me to put on another show. The last thing I felt like doing right then was trying to think up funny stories.

It didn't take long for the shelter to fill back up. A few days after Marge and Boomer had left, police officers arrived with a dozen or so mangy-looking dogs of every size and shape. I overheard some of the volunteers talking. An old man in town wasn't seen for a week or so. When family members went to check up on him, they discovered he had passed away. And they also discovered he had been hoarding animals in his basement—dogs, cats, birds, reptiles, you name it. The place was a zoo.

All of the area shelters were asked to take in as many animals as they could possibly handle. Our shelter took all of the dogs. From what I could tell, there weren't any purebreds, just a bunch of mutts. Now, I have nothing against mutts. I'm not one of those uppity dogs who has a problem with mixed breeds. It was just that this bunch stank to high heaven.

Fortunately, they had come to the right place. In the next 24 hours, they'd all been cleaned up and taken to the vet's office to be checked out. When I had a chance to meet some of the new dogs, I learned they were all fond of their previous owner, but he would sometimes forget to feed them or take them on walks. None of them could remember the last time they had been brushed or combed. It had been a bad way to live, and as much as they wanted to stay together, they knew it was impossible.

They were destined to be split up, but for a chance to go home with a loving and caring family, they were all pretty much on board.

One of the bunch, a lab mix named Rusty, surprised me one day.

"Hey, you," he said.

"Are you talking to me?" I asked.

"Yeah, you. Listen, I hear you're a celebrity."

A celebrity? What was he talking about? Heck, I never considered myself anything but just one of the inmates.

"No, you must be confusing me with someone else," I said.

"I don't think so," he said. "Your name's Rutherford, right?"

I nodded.

"Well, we hear you do a pretty mean stand-up routine. And after what we've been through lately, we could all use a good laugh."

"Where'd you hear that?" I asked.

"Bumped into a greyhound last week who used to be in here. He says you were a stitch."

Uh-oh. Apparently, I'd been exposed. So, now what?

I needed to discourage them. I wasn't confident I could come up with anything funny right now.

"I have been known to tell an occasional funny story," I said. "But I can't think of any just this minute. Sorry."

Rusty rolled his eyes. "One joke? You can't think of one joke? What kind of a stand-up comic are you, anyway?"

Allright, I needed to give this guy something. I closed my eyes and tried to think of what might bring a smile to his face. Within a few seconds, I had something. It wasn't great. Actually, it was average, at best. But it was all I could come up with on short notice.

"So, this policeman walks up to a guy and says, 'Excuse me, sir, it seems your dog's been chasing a boy on a bicycle.' The man appeared confused. He scratched his head. 'Impossible, Officer,' he said. 'It couldn't have been my dog. He can't even ride a bike.'"

The joke, as I expected, had underwhelmed my audience. Half of them didn't even realize I had delivered the punchline. And it didn't help that my wingman, Boomer, wasn't around to supply a timely rim shot.

"So, that's it?" Rusty said. "That's the best you can do." He looked disappointed, and a little ticked off.

"Sorry," I said. There wasn't much else to say.

The expressions of the other dogs said it all. As you might guess, they weren't impressed. And who could blame them? The new arrivals knew nothing about me. It was hardly a good first impression. It was just too bad they couldn't have heard me a week or so ago when Marge and Boomer were still here. I killed. A standing ovation—encore after encore. They had yet to see the real Rutherford, Canine Comic.

"Well, to be perfectly honest," Rusty said, "that was kind of lame…kinda like you." He chuckled. "Get it? Like you? Hey, it looks like *I* oughta be tellin' the jokes around here."

This wasn't the first time another dog had poked fun at me. It had happened before. I would notice some of the others pointing at me and whispering to their friends. Then they would snicker.

But this time, it was worse. This was the first time someone had said it to my face. It hurt.

This was also the first time I had ever really bombed in front of an audience. I had failed at the only thing I was good at. I felt my head begin to droop. I wasn't sure what hurt more—the crack about my legs, or my weak attempt at humor.

Or maybe it wasn't either of those—maybe it was just that my two best friends were gone. The way I felt at that moment, it was possible I had done my last show.

Well, if that was the case, so be it. It was a good run while it lasted. Perhaps it was time for a new career.

Chapter 9

Home Sweet Home

The next couple of weeks seemed to drag. Most of the new residents were still with us, but they had stopped bugging me about putting on one of the famous comedy shows they had heard so much about. They were in no hurry for another weak effort, and I couldn't blame them.

I found myself sleeping most of the time. I didn't seem to have the energy to do much else. Even Vickie commented on my lack of energy. She noticed I was withdrawing from most of the group activities, so she decided to take me to Doc Michaels' clinic to see if there was anything physically wrong with me. They did some blood tests and checked me out. I could have told them it was a waste of time. There's no clinical way to fix a broken heart.

"All the tests were negative," Doc Michaels told Vickie. "He does seem listless, but I can't find anything wrong with him."

"Well, that's good," she said. "I just can't figure it out. Ever since we rescued him, he's been so happy. Then right after Adopt-a-Pet week, things seemed to change."

"You know, that could have something to do with it," Doc Michaels said. "He might be having a difficult time dealing with the turnover at the shelter. Dogs get attached to one another the same way people do."

This doctor was a genius. He knew exactly what was wrong. But there was only one problem—there weren't any pills he could prescribe to help me forget about losing my friends. It would just take time, that was all.

I tried to be optimistic. I could only hope that someday another Marge or Boomer would show up at the rescue center. Now, that would be great. Until then, I'd just have to tough it out.

Things were pretty much the same the next few days. A couple of new dogs arrived, but they were adopted almost immediately. Then, the following week, something occurred I can only describe as life-altering.

I had just awakened from one of my many afternoon naps when the door to the kennel opened, and Vickie walked in. She was followed by a man pushing a boy in a wheelchair. The boy couldn't have been more than ten or eleven years old.

"Here are all the dogs we currently have on hand," she said. "There are some real sweethearts in here."

"We're just hoping to get as lucky as a lady from our church did," the man said. "She got a dog from here a couple of weeks ago, and she just loves her."

"Oh, really?" Vickie said. "Do you remember her name?"

"Mrs. Reynolds. Muriel Reynolds. She lives in our subdivision."

"And what type of dog did she adopt?" Vickie asked.

The little boy sat up in his wheelchair. "It was a collie," he said. "She's pretty old, but she seems like a real nice dog."

Wait a minute! They're talking about Marge. I couldn't believe it. I sure was happy to hear it was all working out. Marge deserved it.

"Listen, I'll let the two of you get acquainted with our little friends here," Vickie said. "If you'd like to play with any of them, let me know, and we'll go into one of our activity rooms." She pointed into the hallway. "I'll be right out there."

"Thanks a lot," the man said.

As Vickie left the room, the man and his son began their official inspection.

"I'm gonna start down there, Dad," the boy said. He grabbed the wheels on his chair and glided down the aisle, passing me on the way. He didn't seem to notice me. So, what else was new?

I watched as the boy and his dad checked out the inhabitants of each cage. When the dad spotted me, he smiled. It was one of those pity smiles. I was used to it. He continued on without saying a word.

When the boy noticed me, his eyes went straight to the cart attached to the rear half of my body. He glanced at his wheelchair and then back at my cart. He paused for a minute, and then moved on to some of the other cages. Before long, he was back. He seemed fascinated by the cart.

Then, he was off. No more than a couple minutes passed, and there he was again—just staring at me. He kept coming back. I wasn't sure why. Maybe he liked me. Or maybe he thought I was some kind of freak.

Although signs overhead warned against it, he put his fingers through the openings in my cage. I walked over and began stiffing him. Since I detected no negative energy, I licked his fingertips. The boy laughed.

"So, what happened to you, pal?" he asked me.

His father strolled over. "Poor little fellow," he said.

"Dad, you said I could pick any dog I wanted, right?"

The dad appeared uneasy. "Well, yeah, I guess I did say that. Why, have you found one you like?"

The little boy pointed directly at me. I couldn't believe it.

His dad crouched down and put his arm around his son. "Adam, you don't really want this dog. You might think you do, but, trust me, you don't"

"Yes, I do," the boy said.

"Son, I don't want you to make a hasty decision. There are a lot of other really nice dogs here. Maybe you should keep looking."

Adam frowned. "You don't like this dog?"

"It's not that I don't like him," the father said. "I'm sure he'd make a great pet. It's just that…"

"Just what?"

His father stood up and sighed. "You need a strong dog who can be your legs. You don't want this one."

"But I do," the boy said. "Dad, look at him. He's just like me. What could be better?"

The father looked frustrated. "I was hoping we'd find a pet that would be perfect for both of us—one to keep you company, and one I could go jogging with. This is not that dog."

Adam folded his arms. He refused to yield. "So, you're holding his disability against him, is that it?"

"No, not exactly."

"Dad, can I ask you a question?"

"Okay," his father said nervously

"Let's just say that I wasn't your son. And you and Mom were looking to adopt a kid. And then you saw me sitting in this wheelchair in some orphanage somewhere. Are you telling me you wouldn't adopt me because of that?"

His father swallowed hard and appeared to tear up. He turned and left the kennel area, only to return with Vickie. They walked over to my cage.

"Could we see this one?" he said, pointing at me.

Vickie looked at Adam and grinned. "You like him, huh?

Adam nodded.

"Ben is one of my favorites," she said. "He's really special. Every so often, I've thought about taking him home myself, but I'm not sure my other three dogs would appreciate that."

We played for a while in the activity room. I was on my best behavior. This was my big chance, and I knew it. Never before had anyone asked to play with me. They probably didn't think I was able to. I needed to convince Adam and his dad I would be the perfect pet.

I licked them whenever it seemed appropriate, although I knew some people weren't big fans of that. I maintained eye contact the entire time. I retrieved a tennis ball and returned it like a good soldier. When Adam picked up a rubber pull toy and held it out to me, we engaged in a spirited game of tug of war. Everything was going great.

Then came my final exam. We went outside to play. I had overheard Adam's dad talking about wanting to run with a dog, and I was ready.

"C'mon, Ben," his dad said as he began to jog down the driveway.

"I hope you can keep up with him, Mr. Sampson," Vickie called out. "He might surprise you."

Adam's dad smiled, but you could see he didn't believe it. I needed to prove myself, and I was more than ready.

I had no problem keeping up with him at first as he jogged down the driveway. Then the pace quickened, but I responded. It was amazing how fast I had gotten with this cart strapped to my back end. It was so easy to pull it along. When Adam's dad shifted into a full sprint, I never missed a beat. It was as if I had become his shadow. He couldn't shake me.

Now, I have to admit I was getting a little tired, but I couldn't show it. I might never get another chance like this again. I had to strut my stuff.

We eventually ended our race at the front door, where Adam was waiting for us. His father bent over and grabbed his sides.

"You passed the test, little guy."

"So, we can get him?" Adam said excitedly.

His dad could only nod. He was too winded to speak.

I don't suppose I have to tell you that this turned out to be the best day of my entire life. While Vickie helped Adam's dad with the paperwork, I stood at attention and awaited my next command. Most of the time, Adam stroked my head, but he really seemed fascinated by my little chariot. He couldn't take his eyes off it.

"This thing is so neat," he said as he rubbed his fingers over the grooves in the tires.

"It is, isn't it?" Vickie said. "And, you know, with that little cart, there's really nothing he can't do. But you should know those casts will be coming off in a few weeks. Then he'll be able to, we hope, walk on his own without the cart."

"Maybe that'll happen for me someday," Adam said. "What do you think, Dad?"

Mr. Sampson forced a smile. "You never know. It could happen."

"Can I ask you a question?" Adam said to Vickie.

"Sure," she said.

He reached down to scratch my ears. "How long has he been named Ben?"

"It's just what we named him when he first came here," Vickie said. "Are you thinking of changing it?"

"I just wondered," Adam said.

Vickie put her finger to her lips in thought. She smiled. "We don't know what his name was before he came here, so, if you'd like to rename him, I'm sure he'll begin to recognize it in no time."

Oh, brother, here we go again, I thought. What was it with humans, anyway? People were always changing our names. I couldn't think of a single instance when a human changed his own name when he got a new dog.

I needed to do something about this. There had to be some way of communicating to Adam that my name was Rutherford. And I'd better figure out a way to do so before he came up with his own new name for me.

"Take your time," his dad said. "This is a big decision—for both of you. Think about it for a couple of days. And in the meantime, we'll just call him Ben. Okay?"

"Okay," Adam said.

It only took Vickie a few more minutes to finish up the paperwork, and then we were in the parking lot as I proudly strutted alongside Adam's wheelchair on my way to their car. We stopped next to a blue-and-beige van. Not a minivan—it was a full-size one. And you wouldn't believe what happened next.

Mr. Sampson opened the side door, pushed a button, and this motorized metal thing started moving toward us. It came straight out of the van to rest on the ground next to Adam, who promptly wheeled his chair up onto it.

I was confused as to what was going on, so I did what all dogs do when we're curious about something. I cocked my head to the side. It always did the trick.

"It's called a lift," Mr. Sampson said. "It helps me get Adam *and* his wheelchair into the van at the same time. Pretty neat, huh?"

It *was* neat.

"We need one for Ben, Dad."

"I think I can manage." Mr. Sampson bent down and lifted me, cart and all, into the van and deposited me at Adam's feet. "I hope he's not one of those dogs who gets carsick."

Adam laughed. "We're about to find out."

Chapter 10
The flame Game

We made it all the way to Adam's house, and I didn't barf once.
Like most dogs, I love riding in the car, especially when the
windows are down. When we pulled into the driveway of
my new home, there was a lady waiting patiently on the front
porch. I assumed it was Adam's mom. She came over to meet
us. She had yellow hair pulled back in a ponytail. She was
really pretty.

"So, let me meet the newest member of the family,"
she said through the open window.

Mr. Sampson jumped out, ran around the van, and approached his wife. He put his arm around her and whispered something. I watched as her expression changed from
a big smile to one of concern.

I had a pretty good idea what he was telling her. Adam's
dad knew she wasn't expecting to see a dog like me. She
was probably hoping for a pet with all its parts in good working order. I didn't want to see the look on her face when

her husband opened the sliding door and she saw me...
and my cart.

I snuggled up close to Adam and waited for the unveiling. I told myself that if she seemed at all unhappy when
she saw my little disability, I would just have to win her
over the same way I did with Mr. Sampson.

Mrs. Sampson nodded and swallowed hard as her husband grabbed the door handle. She was obviously preparing
herself for the worst. As the door slid open, I watched
Adam's face. He didn't seem worried at all. He smiled confidently and scratched my right ear. It was almost as if he
was getting ready to show me off.

When the moment of truth finally arrived, I watched
Adam's parents. Mr. Sampson smiled nervously. His wife
gritted her teeth, expecting the worst.

"So, Mom, what do you think?" Adam said excitedly.

His mom was speechless at first, but when she saw
the grin on Adam's face, I could sense her starting to warm
up to me. Mr. Sampson picked me up and set me on the
driveway. I took that as my cue to meet the wife. I hus-
tled over and stood at attention at her feet. She crouched
down and petted the top of my head. I immediately began licking her hands.

"See, Mom, he likes you," Adam said.

She looked up and smiled. "I guess he does."

Well, I don't have to tell you I was a big hit with the
Mrs. It's tough for the ladies to resist a natural showman,
you know. I think she could see I was special. In no time,
I warmed up to Mrs. Sampson and she warmed up to me.
We got along just great. I could tell she really liked me by
the way she would drop to one knee and scratch behind
my ears. That certainly was one way to win a dog's heart.

The more time I spent with Adam and his parents, the more I knew this was the perfect situation for me. We were all one big happy family. And as a way to thank them for making me an official member of the Sampson clan, I considered it my duty to serve and protect all of them. They may not have thought of me as their faithful and trusty watchdog, but that was okay. I was confident that if I were ever called upon to protect my new family, I would be up to the challenge. Having gone ten rounds with a pack of coyotes, there were very few things that frightened me.

I can't describe how nice it was to be able to stretch my legs any time I wanted. The Sampsons gave me free rein of the property. Adam's dad installed a doggie door at the back entrance to the house. That way, I would be able to come and go as I pleased once I was out of harness. But that made me wonder—How could they be sure I wouldn't just wander away someday?

They discussed putting up a fence around the back yard but decided against it because they were worried the neighbors might object. Then came talk of one of those electrical fences that would give off a shock if I got too close to it. Thank goodness, both Adam and his mom were dead set against that.

In the end, they decided to teach me to stay on their property at all times. I knew that if I was able to convince them I wouldn't wander off into other yards, I'd have the freedom to sneak out every so often.

A month after joining Adam's family, I found myself back at the Stonybrook Animal Hospital. It was the big day—time to have my casts removed. I was back up on the table with the bright light overhead. My cart was on the floor. Doc Michaels spent a few minutes examining my casts.

"Well, it's time for the unveiling," he said. He reached over to a shelf and picked up a strange-looking device. It had a long white handle and a shiny metal wheel at the end. He flipped a switch, and the wheel began spinning really fast.

"What's that?" Adam said.

"It's like a saw," Doc Michaels said. "We need to cut away the casts."

"You won't hurt him, will you?"

"No, don't worry. We cut into it just a little, and then break it away gently. The blade stops if it touches anything soft." He glanced at Adam and his dad. "Is everybody ready?"

They nodded.

While Adam held me down, Doc Michaels began to slice one cast off. I closed my eyes. I kept waiting for the worst, but it never happened. A minute or so later, the doctor turned off the little saw and began to break the cast open. I felt the air hitting my back leg. It felt good. Then he removed the cast from my other leg.

"There we are," Doc Michaels said. "Good as new." He picked me up and set me down on the floor. I was now standing on my four legs...until I fell over.

"Oh, no," Adam said.

"Don't worry, son," Doc Michaels said. "That's perfectly normal. Since he hasn't used them for a few weeks, his back legs are weaker. He'll be a little unsteady for a while. But if you walk him everyday, he'll be back to normal in no time."

"Don't worry," Adam said. "I can do that."

"Let's see if we can get him to walk a little," the doctor said.

Adam wheeled his chair over to the other end of the room. "C'mon, Ben, come over here."

I took a deep breath. I wasn't sure what was going to happen when I put weight on those back legs. *Here we go.*

I stepped forward. I could feel my back end wobble a little. It moved back and forth, and up and down. I took a couple of steps. I was still on my feet.

Mr. Sampson started to laugh. "He's kind of waddling like a penguin."

Hey, that wasn't very nice, I thought. I turned and looked at my back end as I moved. He was right. I *was* walking like a penguin. Another reason I would never be considered watchdog material. Oh, boy.

I kept moving. I fell over a couple of times, but I was able to get right back up on my feet. For the next few minutes, I'd walk a few feet and then stumble. With each step, though, I felt as if my balance was getting a little better. I knew I was walking kind of funny, but it didn't matter to me. I was just happy that I was mobile, sort of.

Everyone in the room started applauding. They were celebrating with me. I had four healthy flippers again. This was gonna be great.

From that point on, everything was just dandy. Adam would faithfully walk me each day. We worked out five minutes the first day. Then ten minutes the next day. Then fifteen minutes the day after that. I could tell my back legs were getting stronger. I wasn't falling over anymore. After a few weeks, I was as good as new. I couldn't believe it.

My new life was a dream come true. If I could just get Adam and his parents to call me by my real name, it would all be perfect. *Ben* wasn't the worst name in the world. I could get used to it, if I had to. But...

That changed the day Adam came home from school with a homework assignment. He had to write a five hundred-word essay about the most interesting American president.

"So, who are you going to write about?" his mother asked.

"I haven't decided yet," he said.

"There are a lot of choices."

"I know," he said. "I don't want to pick the obvious ones—Washington, Lincoln, Jefferson, Roosevelt. All the other kids are doing that. I want to pick one of the lesser-known presidents. Then I might learn something new."

Paula Sampson peeled potatoes over the sink for dinner. "I think that's very smart. And be sure to let me read it when you're done."

"Hey, Mom, does Dad still have that book of presidents somewhere?"

"I think it's in the den on the shelf above the desk," she said. "It's a few years old, you know. I think the last president in the book is Bill Clinton."

"That's okay. I planned to pick one of the older ones anyway...maybe someone from the eighteen-hundreds."

Mrs. Sampson ran cold water over the freshly-peeled potatoes. "Let me know if you need any help."

I followed Adam into the den. It was easy for him to wheel himself from one room to the next. His parents had purposely bought a ranch-style house—that's one where all the rooms are on the same floor. That way there wouldn't be any stairs for him to climb. It sure made my life easier, too. And his folks also had a contractor widen all of the doorways.

"So, who do you think I should write about?" he asked me.

I didn't quite know how to answer that—not that I could anyway.

Adam began looking for the book of presidents. When he spotted it on the shelf, he pulled it down, and began paging through it.

"Okay, Ben, who sounds good?" he said. A minute later, he looked up, closed the book, and set it down on his lap. "I have to tell you the truth. I'm just not sold on that name of yours. We have to come up with something else—something unique." He smiled. "Hey, you know what would be great—if you could somehow tell me what you want to be called." He shook his head and frowned. "But that's impossible, of course." He shrugged. "Oh, well, back to work."

He opened the book to the table of contents. "Try these presidents on for size—and remember, it's got to be somebody who people don't know much about. Let's see… there's John Tyler, James Polk, Zachary Taylor, Millard Fillmore, Franklin Pierce, Rutherford B. Hayes…"

Wait a minute! Did he say Rutherford? Why, that's me. And before Adam could toss out another name, I ran over and started barking.

"Whoa, buddy, what's up?" He set the book down on the desk and immediately wheeled himself over to the window to look out. But there was nothing there. "No dogs or anything. Did you hear something? A cat, or squirrel maybe?" As he wheeled back, he leaned over and stroked my head. "Nothing to worry about." He picked up the book.

"Now, where was I? Oh, yeah, I stopped at Rutherford B. Hayes."

I let out a yelp.

"What's up with you, anyway? What are you trying to tell me?"

He leaned over and began scratching behind my ears. Oh, baby, that felt good. I'm a real sucker for a good ear-scratching. Adam had the perfect touch.

He sat back up and put his finger into the book so as not to lose the page he was on. He seemed to be in deep thought.

"No, it couldn't be," he said. "How could he possibly know…?" He smiled. "Okay, I'm going to try a little experiment." He opened the book. "I was reading these names when you got all excited. Let's try it again. There's John Tyler…James Polk…Zachary Taylor…Millard Fillmore…Franklin Pierce…Rutherford—"

As soon as I heard the name, I started barking and lifted my front paws onto Adam's lap. I didn't know what else to do. I had to make him know my real name was Rutherford, and that was what I wanted him to call me.

"It's just not possible," he said. He stared right at me. "John Tyler."

I didn't move a muscle. This would be perfect. He was playing right into my paws.

"James Polk."

I just stared. No reaction.

"Zachary Taylor."

I tried to appear totally disinterested.

"Millard Fillmore."

I yawned for effect.

"Franklin Pierce?"

I pretended I was falling asleep.

"Rutherford—"

I howled and began patting Adam's hands with my paws.

He shook his head. "It's almost as if you know what I'm saying. Are you trying to tell me I should write my paper on Rutherford B. Hayes?"

No! No! No! That wasn't it at all. I couldn't care less who he wrote about. I couldn't believe it. We were so close.

Adam stared forward. "Wait a minute. Are you saying you want me to *call* you Rutherford?"

I began nodding. There was no way he could confuse that with anything else.

He dropped the book to the floor. He was dumbfounded. He cradled my head in his hands.

"I'm either going nuts, or you're the smartest dog in the world." He thought for a few seconds. "Okay," he said. "Let's try something." He picked up my paws and gently set them down on the floor. He pointed at me. "Now, you stay right there." He then proceeded to wheel himself across the room and spun around to face me. "Here we go. Do or die." He clapped his hands loudly. "Come here, *Ben*. Come on, *Ben*."

For just a second, I began to lunge forward. It was instinct. But fortunately, I was able to resist the urge to move my feet.

"Interesting," he said. "Now for the moment of truth." He smiled. "Come here, *Rutherford*."

I sprinted over to him and began licking his hands.

"Well, that's it," Adam announced. "From this day forward, you will officially be known as *Rutherford*. Is that okay with you, pal?"

I barked my approval. I almost couldn't believe this was happening. I mean—how many dogs do you know who actually get to pick their own names? This had to be a first.

"Come on, buddy, let's go tell Mom."

I followed him out of the den and back into the kitchen. His mom was loading the dishwasher.

"Hey, Mom, guess what?" he said.

"What's that?"

"I've finally decided what name to give…" He pointed at me. "Him."

Mrs. Sampson leaned against the counter and folded her arms. "So, *Ben* is out, huh?"

"He doesn't look like a Ben," he said. "And I'll bet he never even liked that name."

His mother smiled. "So, what should I call him now?"

Adam sat up in his wheelchair and proudly let loose. "His name is…Rutherford."

The expression on his mom's face was a cross between confusion and disbelief.

"Rutherford? Honey, what kind of a name is that for a dog?"

"Don't blame me," Adam said, motioning in my direction. "*He* picked it."

She placed her hands on her hips. "*He* picked it?"

"Yeah," Adam said. "I was trying to figure out what president to do my report on so I just started rattling off a bunch of names. And then every time I said the name *Rutherford,* for Rutherford B. Hayes, he went crazy."

Mrs. Sampson shook her head in disbelief. "Really?"

"Mom, I'm telling you the truth. He won't even answer to the name Ben anymore.

"Well, we'll just see about that," she replied as she opened up a cabinet, grabbed a box of dog treats, and began shaking it.

Oh, boy. Be still my heart. This wasn't fair. She was playing dirty.

I had to control my urges. I had to fight. I kept telling myself that self-control would pay off in the long run. Pass up a treat now, and there'll be plenty to choose from once they see how responsive I am to the name *Rutherford*.

Adam's mom dug into the box for a tasty treat. She crouched down and waved it around.

"Come over here, *Ben*. Look what I have for you."

My legs wanted to sprint over and devour that chewy liver-cheese-bacon-flavored morsel, but I couldn't. I just couldn't. My legs started to shake. My entire body was trembling. I *could* do this. I *would* do this.

I locked my jaw and tried to think about chasing squirrels and drinking from the toilet—anything that would take my mind off that treat. She just kept waving it. She probably was confident she could break me.

But that would never happen. Considering what I had been through in the past few months—Horace, the coyotes, the accident—it would take more than a simple dog treat, even though it was almost irresistible, for me to cave in. I dug in my paws for the standoff.

A moment later, she looked over at Adam and shook her head.

"I can't believe this." She smiled at me and sighed. "Okay, here goes," she said. "Come here, *Rutherford*, look what I have for you."

It was music to my ears. I put my head down and made a mad dash for Mrs. Sampson. But at the last second, when I attempted to put on the brakes, I realized that a shiny, slippery kitchen floor doesn't offer the best footing. I started to slide…and slide…and slide…right into her, knocking her over onto the floor.

Oh, no, would she be upset? Would she hate me? Would she have me banished?

I soon realized I had nothing to worry about. Not only did none of those things happen, but what did couldn't have been better. Mrs. Sampson started to laugh. She actually laughed. She didn't seem upset with me at all.

And then Adam started laughing. So, I figured—why not join the party? I jumped up and put my front paws on his lap. Then I started licking his face. It was all good.

When Adam's dad got home that night, he had a hard time believing I had picked out my own name, and he had an even harder time believing the name I had chosen. But when he saw me ignore any commands containing the name *Ben*, and then saw how excited I got when he referred to me as *Rutherford*, it didn't take him long to buy in as well.

I couldn't ever remember being any happier. I was in a real home, with a loving family, and people would now call me by my real name. It didn't get any better than this.

The end.

Well, not quite. My story doesn't end here, although it might seem like a perfect place for it. My job wasn't over. And my bad habit of mixing it up with nasty people and critters had only just begun.

©brad w. foster 2020

Chapter 11

The Price of Success

On the weekend, Adam and his dad decided to take me out for a little exercise, and to see how well I'd get along with other dogs. When we pulled into the parking lot, I immediately sensed a commotion. The barking was deafening.

I lifted my head and peeked out the window. I couldn't believe what I was looking at. Was this another kind of shelter? An outdoor one, maybe? What was the deal with all these dogs?

My question was soon answered.

"So, what do you think?" Adam said as he stroked the top of my head. "If you're wondering where we are, this place is called a *dog park*. It's where guys like you can run around to your heart's content."

"And off-leash," his dad said.

I stared at both of them, then back at the other dogs.

As we made our way from the parking lot, Adam's expression began to change.

114

"Dad, there's an awful lot of barking going on. I don't like the sound of it. Suppose one of those dogs attacks Rutherford. What'll we do? He's not the kind of dog who can defend himself very well."

"We'll keep a real close eye on him," Mr. Sampson said. "And I wouldn't worry. People aren't supposed to let their dogs run free if they don't get along with other dogs. I'm sure he'll be just fine."

I tended to agree. I could tell by the tone of the barking this was a friendly environment. It was what you might call "happy to meet you" barking, as opposed to "get out of my face" barking. The two aren't anything alike.

The body language was friendly as well. Here's something to remember. If a dog's tail is wagging, you're usually fine. But if they snap their teeth, then you had better look out. And if they raise their body and you see that their tail and ears are straight up, then it's time to take cover.

I took a good look at my fellow canines running around in the park. I didn't immediately notice anyone who might be considered dangerous. Before my unfortunate encounter with the truck on the highway, I would have been nervous about confronting a violent animal. With my bad back leg, I was slower than most other dogs, and since the accident, I'm still a little slower on the run, even more than before.

Adam held tightly onto my leash as we entered the park. Like a new mother watching her little one march off on the first day of school, he seemed reluctant to let me go.

"He'll be fine, Adam," his dad said. "Don't worry."

"But what if some of the dogs gang up on him?"

"I doubt if that'll happen. But if it does, I'll run right over and scoop him up."

"It makes me nervous not to have him on a leash. What if he gets lost? Then what'll we do?"

His dad smiled. "Adam, relax, there's a fence all the way around this park. There's no way he could get out."

"But what if some dog dug a hole under the fence that nobody knows about? Then what?"

Mr. Sampson shook his head. "Well, I guess now's as good a time as any." He jogged back to the car. When he returned a minute later, he was holding something in his hand. He crouched down and slid this funny-looking collar around my neck.

"Dad, what's that?"

"That is an insurance policy."

"Huh?"

His dad chuckled. "Well, not exactly. But it's a guarantee that we'll never lose Rutherford." He snapped the collar in place and pushed and activated a button on it. "There. We're all set."

"Dad, what's going on?"

Mr. Sampson stood up and placed his hand on his son's shoulder. "Adam, you know that directional device in the car that tells us which way to go when we're headed someplace new?"

"You mean the GPS?"

"This little gadget is a GPS for dogs. Wherever he goes, we'll always know where he is."

"So, is there a little screen for it, too?"

Adam's dad pulled a cell phone from his pocket, tapped on the screen, and held it up so they both could see it.

"See that little red dot that's flashing? Notice where it is?"

"On Center Street," Adam said.

"And where's the dog park?"

Adam thought for a moment, then threw his arms into the air. "On Center Street!" he exclaimed. "This is amazing."

His dad laughed. "So, now, will you please let Rutherford go play with the other dogs?"

Adam grinned and unhooked the leash. I immediately took that as my cue. I set my sights on the far end of the park and let loose

You should have seen the stares from all the other dogs when they got a good look at the way I ran—up and down, left to right—just like a penguin. Their jaws dropped. It was clear that none of them had ever seen a dog with two bum legs pass by them. The ground, I must say, was a bit bumpy. I wasn't ready for some of the uneven stretches. But that was fine. I'd put up with a few bumps for a chance to run around and make some new friends.

Every so often, I'd glance over my shoulder. As expected, Adam had his eye on me. I knew he'd never let me out of his sight. I was okay with that. I didn't expect any trouble but if someone or something did happen to make some trouble, it was nice to know the cavalry was only a few yards away.

When I reached the far end of the park, I was delighted I wasn't out of breath in the least. I always took pretty good care of myself—daily exercise whenever I got a chance and no junk food. Of course, if anyone had ever bothered to offer me a little junk food, I don't even want to think of what kind of shape I might be in. As you may have noticed, most dogs have little to no will power. Put anything other than a fruit or vegetable in front of us, and stand back.

I put in a couple more lengths of the park before taking a break. Each day I could feel my back legs getting stronger. In no time, I'd be back to my old self.

I decided I had earned the chance to stop and socialize a little. I began approaching various packs of dogs who were just shooting the breeze. I didn't barge in or anything. I waited for an invitation. After four or five encounters with different groups, it soon became obvious that no one had any intention of asking me to join their little cliques.

But why? What was wrong with me? I knew I was the new guy, but all these other dogs were new at one time. And I was aware my back end swayed from one side to the other, but that was no big deal. Was it? I wasn't sure why the others were so reluctant to invite me into their inner circle.

After about ten minutes of trying to infiltrate the various groups, I gave up and headed back to where Adam and his dad were waiting for me. I knew I'd always get a welcome reception from them.

I was only a few feet away from rejoining my faithful owners when I heard a familiar voice.

"It can't be. It just can't be. Is that you? Is that really you, Rutherford?"

When I turned to look, I couldn't believe my eyes. Standing before me was Marge.

"Marge?" I said. I ran over, and we rubbed noses. It was so great to see her. "I never thought I'd see you again." I said.

"Me neither," she said. "So, you're on the outside now. Did you get adopted?"

I nodded.

"Rutherford, I am so happy for you. I knew this would happen someday."

"You had a lot more faith than I did," I said. "I was expecting to live out the rest of my days in the shelter."

"I knew the right family would eventually come along." She looked around. "So, where are they?"

I pointed toward Adam and his dad. I wondered what she would think when she saw Adam's wheelchair, but she didn't say a thing.

"Just look at you. You're back on all fours. No more cart. That must feel great."

"It does," I said. I was going to make a comment about my funny way of walking since my casts came off, but I knew it wouldn't matter to Marge.

"Hey, you haven't seen Boomer around, have you? Was he still in the shelter when you left?"

"You won't believe this," I said with a grin, "but he got adopted, too." My smile quickly faded.

"What's wrong?"

"To tell you the truth, I didn't think much of the guy who adopted him."

"What do you mean?"

"Well, he was…you know…kind of odd."

"Odd in what way?" she asked.

"He just looked mean. And I couldn't figure out why he'd want a dog like Boomer. He didn't talk to him or play with him. He saw this timid little guy under the towel, and then he said, 'I'll take him.' Just like that."

Marge could sense my concern. "Maybe he works with frightened dogs. Maybe he rehabilitates them. You never know." She always tended to look for the silver lining.

I shrugged.

"Well, let's just hope we bump into him someday," she said. "Then we can find out for ourselves how he's doing."

Before Marge and I could continue our conversation, another dog walked up.

"Rutherford? I thought that was you. How the heck are you doing?" It was the greyhound from the shelter. He was a big fan of my stand-up routine.

"I'm doing good," I said.

"I was just talking to Marge a few days ago and wondering whatever happened to you," he said.

"Well, now you know."

He leaned in and smiled. "Hey, do you think you could do your act here in the dog park for all of the regulars? I know they'd love it."

Was he kidding? I hadn't performed in public for weeks. I couldn't just think up a whole routine off the top of my head.

"I'll tell you what," he said. "I'll round up a few of the fellas. That'll give you time to think up a few good jokes. See you in a couple of minutes." And with that, he was off.

I stared at Marge, dumbfounded. "He's not serious, is he?"

"Your reputation has preceded you, I'm afraid," she said.

"So, what do I do now? I can't come up with something that quick."

"You know, Rutherford, you always say that, but then you manage to think up some really good stuff. I saw you do it at the shelter a dozen times or more." She offered a half-smile. "Think hard. I'll bet you can put something together if you try."

Oh, brother, the pressure was really on this time. The last thing I wanted to do was to make a bad first impression. I needed some killer stuff. I didn't want to disappoint these guys. I was hoping to come here with Adam as often as possible, and if I bombed, I might not be welcomed back.

"I'm gonna head over there by that clump of trees and try to think of something," I said.

"Okay," Marge said. "I'll stall them as long as I can."

"Thanks." I looked over my shoulder at Adam and his dad. They were talking to some other owners. Good. I needed a little time.

I immediately headed to the far end of the park to work my magic. I wasn't particularly confident I could do this, but I had to try. Since some of these guys were former shelter dwellers, I'd need some new material. That would prove to be a challenge, but what else could I do?

When I finally made it to the clump of trees, I sat down under a maple and tried to concentrate. It wasn't easy with all the noise around. I closed my eyes and tried to block out everything else. A minute later, I was in my own little world. I didn't hear a thing.

I tried to recall which jokes I had never used at the shelter. I tried to remember some of my favorites from past performances at the breeding farm. And I tried to think up some new material—the toughest of all when you're pressed for time.

When I finally opened my eyes, I realized that several minutes had passed. The greyhound, whose name I learned was Gus, was hovering over me.

"Are you okay?" he said. "For a minute there, I thought you were dead. I kept calling your name, but you didn't answer."

"Sorry," I said. "I was deep in thought. I haven't done a stand-up routine for a few weeks. I needed time to come up with some new material."

"So, have you got some killer stuff for us?" Gus said.

I smiled weakly. "Well, I've got something. I hope you like it."

He winked and put one of his front paws on my shoulder. "C'mon, it's showtime."

I followed Gus over to where the other dogs were waiting. When we got there, I was surprised to see the turnout. I was expecting two or three, at best, but there had to be more than twenty dogs eagerly waiting for my routine.

"So, would you like me to introduce you?" Gus asked.

"No, I don't think that'll be necessary," I said. "There's someone else here who can do the honors." I looked at Marge. "Would you mind?"

She grinned. "Not at all. It'd be my pleasure."

She turned to the audience and began barking. Then, once everyone had quieted down, she did her thing.

"Ladies and gentlemen, it gives me great pleasure to present a sensational new member of our group. This entertainer comes to us from a three-month engagement at the Bardmoor Rescue Center, where he performed to standing room-only crowds each and every night. So, let's give a nice dog-park welcome to Rutherford, Canine Comic."

Marge had to have been a professional announcer in another life. Nobody, and I mean nobody, could warm up a crowd like her. I waited for the applause to die down before I dove in.

"Thanks, Marge, and thanks to all of you for such a warm welcome. It's great to be here." I paused momentarily and glanced skyward. "Hmmm, a little overcast. In a few minutes, it could be raining cats and dogs. Be careful not to step in any poodles."

At first there was no reaction. But then a Great Dane in the back let out a roar.

"Good one, kid."

Whew. I continued.

"I got this buddy…an old English sheepdog…nice guy but really dumb."

"How dumb is he?" Marge yelled out, right on cue.

"He's so dumb, he chases parked cars."

A few more chuckles followed.

"Hey, did you hear the one about the cowboy who decided to buy a dachshund. It seems he wanted to get a long little doggie." I waited for laughter, but there was none. I found myself looking into a sea of confused faces. Apparently, they needed a little help. "Get it? 'Get *along, little dogey*'?"

A second later, the smiles were visible. The Great Dane let out a belly laugh. "Keep 'em coming, Rutherford. You're on a roll."

I grinned. I could tell they were warming up to me.

"So, this guy walked into a little country store and noticed a sign that said: *Beware of Dog!* in big bold letters. Then he spotted this harmless old hound dog asleep on the floor next to the cash register. So, he asked the store manager, 'Is that the dog people are supposed to beware of?' 'Yep, that's him,' the manager replied.

"The man smiled. 'He certainly doesn't look like a dangerous dog to me. Why in the world did you post that sign?'

"'Dangerous?' the manager said. 'Who said anything about dangerous? I put up the sign because people kept tripping over him.'"

I made the rimshot sound with my mouth. It seemed to work. A bunch of them started laughing right away.

Marge leaned over. "I gotta learn how to make that sound for you. I'll work on it."

It was time to send the crowd home with smiles on their faces. I needed a really good one to close the show.

"Hey, did you hear about the man who went on a safari to Africa and took his pet schnauzer with him for company?

"Well, one day the schnauzer is out chasing butterflies, and before long he gets himself lost. A few minutes later, he sees a leopard running after him at full speed. If he doesn't think of something fast, he's about to become someone's lunch.

"He notices some bones on the ground a few feet away. He turns his back to the approaching cat and begins chewing on the bones. Then, just as the leopard is about to pounce, he yells out, 'Boy, that was one delicious leopard. I wonder if there are any more around here.'

"Hearing this, the leopard stops in his tracks, and he slinks away into the jungle. 'Whew,' says the leopard. 'That was close. That schnauzer nearly had me.'

"Meanwhile, a monkey who's been watching the whole scene from a nearby tree figures he can put this knowledge to good use and trade it for protection from the leopard. So, off he goes. The schnauzer sees him heading after the leopard, and figures something must be up.

"The monkey soon catches up with the leopard, spills the beans about what had actually happened. The leopard is furious at being made a fool of and says, 'Okay, monkey, hop on my back, and let's take care of that conniving canine.'

"Minutes later, the schnauzer sees the leopard running toward him with the monkey on his back. *What am I going to do now?* he thinks.

"Then, instead of running, the dog sits down with his back to his attackers, pretending he hasn't seen them yet. When they get close enough to hear, the schnauzer says, 'Where's that darn monkey? I sent him off half an hour ago to bring me another leopard.'"

I waited a second and hoped for the best. And let me tell you, it was worth waiting for. The entire audience was in stitches. They were beside themselves. Some were laughing so hard they fell over. Others started to tear up. I had saved my best for last.

Now I had to give them the bad news that the show was over. I looked at Marge and motioned for her to join me.

"Needless to say, you're a hit," she said.

"Thanks, but I'm also outta jokes. Do you suppose you could break the news to the audience?"

"Not a problem." Marge began barking in an effort to quiet down the masses. A moment later, she had their attention. "Thanks so much for coming. I hope you enjoyed the show. We'll be sure to let you know when Rutherford's next performance will be scheduled." She waved her paw at the crowd. "Until next time, people."

"Wait a minute," a malamute in the back row said. "The show's over? He was just getting started. He can't stop now."

A border collie chimed in. "Aw, c'mon. One more. Please."

"I'm not leavin' till he tells another joke," a boxer said.

"That goes for me, too," a black lab echoed.

I didn't know what to do. I was clean out of jokes. And with everyone staring at me, there was no way I'd be able to think up any new material. I looked for Adam. I needed him to rescue me, but he and his dad were at least fifty yards away. They had no idea I was in a jam.

The boxer folded his front paws. "I'm waiting."

The malamute chimed in. "One more joke won't kill you."

Gus the greyhound stepped out from the crowd and faced what had suddenly become an angry mob.

"Listen, people, be reasonable. Rutherford didn't even know he'd be performing today. He threw together that routine in a matter of minutes. He'll put on another show real soon, but you gotta be patient."

"That's all well and good," the boxer said. "But I ain't movin' till he tells at least one more joke. Got it?"

Marge stepped directly in front of me, trying to shield me from the crowd. I appreciated her help, but if things suddenly got ugly, we were in big trouble. Marge was too old to protect herself, let alone me.

She reached back with her front paw and pulled me closer to her. Whatever was about to happen, at least we would face it together.

Chapter 12

Ace in the Hole

Just when I was convinced success would also be my downfall, a strange thing happened. From the back of the crowd, I spotted the Great Dane muscling his way to the front. When he reached the spot where Marge and I were standing, he narrowed his eyes and stared daggers at the others.

"You were told in no uncertain terms the show is over," he said. "Do I have to refresh your memories?"

The crowd of dogs that a minute ago had been demanding an encore immediately quieted down and began to wander off. They weren't happy about having been sent away, but it was clear they had no intentions of tangling with a dog his size.

The Dane turned and smiled. "The name's Ace. Nice to meet you, Rutherford."

I extended my paw, and we shook. "I don't know how to thank you," I said.

"Don't worry about it," Ace said. "I saw a fellow canine in need and decided to lend a hand. That's all there was to it."

"Well, thanks again," I said.

"If you don't mind, can I ask you a question?" Ace said.

"Sure."

"What are you going to do the next time this happens, and I'm not around to save the day?"

Marge smiled. "I don't think we were in any real danger. Some of these folks get a little impatient at times, but I can't imagine any of them actually harming us. They would eventually have gotten tired of waiting and would have gone home."

"Don't be so sure," Ace said. "I've seen what can happen when a crowd gets ugly. And, trust me, it ain't pretty."

I didn't want to say it, but I wasn't as confident as Marge that everything would have worked out just fine. I had been really afraid.

Ace winked at me. "Marge is probably right. I don't suppose anyone in that crowd would actually have tried to rough you up." He turned to leave. "At least, I hope not. Good luck, kid. It looks like you're gonna need it."

I didn't like the way he had said that. Maybe he was right. Maybe these crowds could get ugly. And then what would I do?

"Excuse me, Ace," I said. "Do you have any ideas on how we can avoid situations like this in the future?"

The Great Dane stopped in his tracks. He turned and smiled. "I'm glad you asked," he said. "I have just the answer for you."

"Really?"

He sat down next to us. "What you need, kid, is an agent. That would solve all your problems."

"An agent?" I asked. "What's that?"

I noticed the look on Marge's face. She seemed skeptical.

"Every entertainer who's worth his weight has an agent," Ace said. "How would you like having someone to book all your performances in advance, and who would make sure you had plenty of time to think up new material? How would you like having someone to handle crowd control—someone who could untangle situations like the one today when things get a little unruly? And how would you like getting *paid* for your performances?"

"Paid?"

"Kid, you're giving away the product. And that product has value," Ace said. "If these guys want to hear a stand-up routine, they oughta pay for it."

I had never considered charging for my shows. Was I even good enough to expect payment for telling a few jokes? I wasn't sure.

"You actually think other dogs would pay to hear me do what I do?" I said.

"And just where do you expect dogs to get money to pay for a show?" Marge said. She wasn't buying it.

Ace chuckled. "Who said anything about money?"

I was confused.

"Your adoring fans will pay with something far better than money. I'm talking about *treats*—and good ones. Imagine rawhide bones, bacon bites, chicken, lamb, or beef biscuits—even peanut butter treats."

I couldn't believe what I was hearing. Was this really possible? I licked my lips. Suddenly, I was famished.

Marge scratched her head. "I don't know," she said. "I'm trying to imagine a dog actually saving a treat, and then giving it away to pay for a comedy show. It just doesn't sound like any dogs I've ever known."

Ace's expression soured. "They'll do it. You'll see. Have you ever seen how a squirrel collects food and then stores it away for the winter? It's the same thing."

"But dogs are different," Marge argued. "We don't think like that. When we see a treat, we think about one thing —how fast can we get it into our bellies."

"I'll tell you what," Ace said. "Try out this agent thing for a week, and if it's not everything I said it was, then you can walk away. What do you say?"

I glanced at Marge. I knew she wasn't too keen on the idea, but I wasn't sure if she had issues with the business arrangement or with Ace.

"So *you'd* be Rutherford's agent? Is that what you're saying?" Marge asked.

He nodded.

"And what do you get out of it?" she said.

"The standard fifteen-percent agency commission," he said. "No more, no less."

Marge shrugged. "It's up to you, Rutherford."

I just couldn't see a downside. Having somebody else book all of my performances well in advance, and giving me plenty of time to come up with new material, seemed like a no-brainer. Adding a little muscle to deal with an unruly crowd made perfect sense. Not to mention the bacon bites and all the other treats. And if things didn't work out, I could walk away in a week's time. What did I have to lose?

"I'll do it!" I said.

"That's great. Just great," Ace said. "You won't regret it."

Marge rolled her eyes. "I'm just not convinced this is necessary."

"No disrespect, ma'am," Ace said, "but you're not the one who has to keep track of multiple bookings. You're not the one who has to wrack his brain to think up new jokes. And you're not the one who has to fend off a bloodthirsty crowd."

"Bloodthirsty?" she said. "I don't think—"

"It's not your call," Ace said. "Rutherford's already made up his mind. Right, kid?"

"Well, yeah, I guess so."

Ace patted me on the back. "Good boy. I'll put the contract together and stop by tomorrow for your signature." He winked. "Trust me. You won't be sorry." He smiled at me, glared at Marge, and was soon on his way.

🐾🐾🐾

The next few weeks were a blur. Things were happening so quickly I had a hard time keeping track of them.

As promised, Ace dropped by the house the next day with the contract. There was so much legalese in it I wasn't exactly sure what I was signing. I asked him if I could have Marge look at it, since she knew a lot about the law, but Ace assured me it was standard contract language and that I had nothing to worry about. He also came prepared with a ten-page business plan.

I soon learned he intended to book me at doggie birthday parties, doggie graduations, doggie anniversaries—basically any kind of gathering that brought dogs together. He had recruited his own staff of worker bees…or rather, worker dogs, who spread the word about me and my talents all over the neighborhood.

A week later, I was working my first paid gig—an engagement party for a pair of Boston terriers who lived down the block. It was just the first of many. The bookings were nonstop for the first few weeks, but Ace always made sure I had at least three days between each show to come up with fresh material.

That helped, but the strain was getting to me. I wasn't sure how much longer I'd be able to continue at this pace.

Soon, my reputation had reached far and wide. Everyone knew who I was. I couldn't walk down the street without being recognized. There was a downside, however. I had been so busy with stand-up jobs that I had very little time for my old friends. I hadn't seen a familiar face in weeks. And when I did, there wasn't time for anything but a wave, and usually there wasn't even time for that.

I missed hanging out with my friends. I'd thought that performing all the time and getting paid for it would be the ideal situation, but I was beginning to have my doubts.

As time went on, I couldn't help but notice my new celebrity status was different from the one I had enjoyed at the breeding farm or at the shelter. All the dogs in the neighborhood said hello, but it was more of a polite hello instead of a friendly hello., I didn't think much of it until I bumped into Marge one day at the dog park.

"How are you, Rutherford?" She seemed a little distant. "I haven't seen you in…at least a month, I'd say."

"I'm sorry about that, Marge. My schedule's really been crazy the last few weeks. Ace has me doing two to three gigs a week. And when I'm not on stage, I'm working on new material. It's been nuts, let me tell you."

"Well, I'm glad things are working out. It looks like I was wrong. Apparently, you did need an agent."

By the way she was acting, I could tell something was different. Marge wasn't her usual warm, friendly self. She never once looked me in the eye when she spoke. I moved a little closer, hoping for one of her famous hugs, but there was none.

"Is anything wrong?" I asked.

"Wrong? Why would you say that?"

"You seem…different. That's all."

"*I* seem different?" Marge sighed. "Rutherford, can I be frank?"

I nodded.

"There's nothing wrong with me. It's you. You're the one who's changed."

"What are you talking about?" I said. I didn't want to sound defensive, but it was hard not to.

"Can't you see what's going on? You're not the same happy, innocent, fun-loving Rutherford anymore."

So, how was that my fault? I was just trying to honor the contract. It seemed pretty clear Marge didn't understand the demands of being a celebrity.

Did she think this was easy? Handling the pressure of multiple stand-up performances a week was brutal. And what about having to think up new material every couple of days? Apparently, she had never heard of writer's block. Let me tell you—it was torture. Maintaining a schedule like mine was stressful. Why couldn't she see that?

"My schedule might have changed," I said, "but I haven't."

"Haven't you?"

I didn't think so, but maybe I had and didn't realize it. "What, exactly, seems different about me?"

Marge sat down next to me and shook her head.

"Rutherford, I'm afraid that success has gone to your head. You seem too good for your friends now. You don't treat us like friends anymore. You treat us like customers—paying customers. And if we're not willing to pay, then we're no longer a part of your life."

"Those aren't my rules," I said. "That's how Ace works things."

Marge smiled. "We miss you—the *old* you."

I didn't know what to say. When I agreed to take on an agent and get paid to perform, I never thought it would affect relationships with my friends. I thought I'd have time for both, but I guess I was wrong. I hadn't realized the time commitment necessary to handle the job. Maybe it was time to rethink what was important to me.

"I'm sorry about all of this," I said. "This isn't the way it was supposed to be."

"I remember when you first came to the shelter," she said. "You just wanted to fit in. You just wanted to make friends. You just wanted to be part of the gang.

"And when we found out about your joke-telling talent, you became a real hit. You seemed to enjoy telling funny stories because you knew the other dogs would love hearing them, not because anyone was paying you to do it." She lifted my head with her paw.

"I could be wrong," she said. "You seem happy about your success, but you *are* different. And you have to believe me when I say I would never stand in your way if I thought this was the best thing for you. But I don't."

She smiled weakly. "And please don't think I'm jealous. This has nothing to do with your newfound popularity, or with the hundreds of dog treats you must now have."

I chuckled. "To tell you the truth, I have more dog treats than I'll ever need. Adam doesn't know it, but I've stashed most of them under his bed. And I'm running out of room."

Marge leaned over and hugged me. Boy, had I missed those hugs.

"I loved it at the shelter with you and Boomer," I said. "Those were some of the best days of my life. And even though I was thrilled to get adopted, sometimes I actually miss that place. Things were just simpler back then." Out of the corner of my eye, I could see Ace running toward us.

"What are you doing?" he said. "You don't have time for idle chatter. You've got a puppy shower tomorrow afternoon. I hope you've worked up a routine for them. You can't expect to use any of your retreads, you know."

Marge looked at me, shook her head, and turned away.

"Wait, Marge," I said, but she kept walking and didn't look back.

Chapter 13
No Minors Allowed

The next month was just as hectic as the last—two to three performances a week and never a minute to call my own. I was straining to come up with new material. I wouldn't say writer's block had set in. It had more to do with the fact there was simply a limited supply of dog jokes out there.

Over the past few weeks, I had cranked out funny dog stories about just about every known breed; stories about strange or eccentric owners; stories about fights with cats, squirrels, and chipmunks; kennel disasters; groomer goofs —you name it. There were only so many humorous situations a typical dog might find himself in.

I asked Ace one day to give me more time between performances so I could come up with new material, but he just shook his head, rolled his eyes, and told me to follow him. I had no idea where we were going. He didn't say a word the entire time.

We walked through a couple of neighborhoods I wasn't familiar with. Then, in the distance, I could see the dog park. I now had a pretty good idea where I was.

He went into a clump of trees and began looking around. It was almost as if he was making sure no one was watching us. When he was certain we were alone, he walked up to a large oak tree and began digging right next to it. He dug furiously for a couple of minutes, then suddenly stopped.

I leaned in to see what was in the bottom of the hole. It was a bunch of papers all rolled up. He pulled out one, glanced at it, and tossed it back in. He did that a couple more times before finding what he was looking for.

He unrolled the paper, smiled, and handed it to me. I recognized it immediately. It was the contract I had signed making Ace my agent. He pointed to my signature, and then to a clause where I had promised to do a minimum of ten shows per month. I hadn't recalled seeing that before. I sighed. I was stuck. There was nothing I could do.

As the weeks went by, I found myself spending less and less time with Adam and his family. Every time his dad wanted me to go with him on a run, I would have to come up with an excuse for not going. And it wasn't like I could just tell him I was too busy. I had to communicate it in a way a human could understand.

Sometimes I would pretend I was asleep or too tired. Other times I would lift one of my front paws and make it seem as if it hurt to walk on it. That would always guarantee a little me-time, but I felt guilty because I really enjoyed running alongside him while he jogged. It was great to get out in the fresh air and explore some new surroundings, not to mention all the things to sniff at.

Every time I'd get overwhelmed, I'd start thinking about what Marge had said to me at the dog park. I hated to admit it, but it appeared she was right. I *had* changed—and not for the better. I was busy all the time, either writing or performing. I couldn't remember the last time I had played with any of my friends. I had a fulltime job.

And although I was now a celebrity, I couldn't really say I was any happier. I was successful. Darned successful. All you had to do was look under Adam's bed at the stash of dog treats.

But what good was all of that without happiness?

I found myself thinking about my mother a lot. I really missed talking to her, and especially nuzzling up to her. She was always so warm and cuddly. And if I ever had a problem, she was always there to help me work through it. If she were here right now, I wondered what advice she might give me.

But the more I thought about it, the more I realized I didn't need my mother or Marge or anyone else to tell me what to do. This was an easy decision.

The happiest I had ever been was when Adam and his family adopted me. It was something I had dreamed about all my life. And I'd always enjoyed telling an occasional funny story. It made me feel good to hear them laugh. Now that it had become a job, the fun was gone.

I knew then and there what I had to do. I had to explain to Ace that I wanted out of the contract. I would tell him I appreciated all his hard work, but that I was no longer interested in charging other dogs to hear my jokes. I might be "giving away the product", as he said, but that was perfectly fine with me.

It had never bothered me before. It wasn't as if I'd felt like I was being cheated or anything. The only payment I'd ever needed was the laughter I got from a well-timed punchline.

Just thinking about giving up paid performances and returning to the way things used to be made me smile. What a relief it would be to give up this hectic schedule.

I knew getting out of the contract wasn't going to be easy. Ace wouldn't be happy. He would try to talk me out of it. He might even try to force me to honor it. If that happened, I wasn't sure what I would do.

I knew one thing for sure—I didn't want to face him alone.

The next day, while Adam was at school, I snuck out and went over to visit Marge. I told her about my decision to give up the stage. She was thrilled. And the best news was that she agreed to be at my side when I broke the news to Ace.

"I don't want you to rush into anything because of what I said," she told me.

"Listen, Marge, if I really loved this new career, I would never give it up. It's my call. I guess I'm just not cut out to be a celebrity."

"That's just it," she said. "You're still a celebrity. You don't need to charge other dogs to hear you tell jokes to make you a celebrity. You were a fan favorite before you ever had an agent. That will never change."

"Really?"

"You'll always be Rutherford, Canine Comic, and don't you forget it."

I was so glad to hear her say that. And with Marge by my side, I wasn't afraid of confronting Ace.

We decided to head for the dog park. There was a good chance he would be there. We knew he often did business deals at the park.

On the way, Marge kept telling me how good it would be to have me back the way I used to be. She didn't like seeing me work so hard. She didn't like that I had abandoned my friends. And she didn't much like Ace. That was apparent.

When we entered the dog park, we spotted Ace talking to a pair of poodles. When we got closer, I heard him offering to help manage their modeling careers. When he spotted us, he held up his paw for us to wait. We were able to overhear part of the conversation.

"And all I ask is a measly fifteen percent," he told the poodles. "It's a standard agent's commission."

I knew I should have kept my nose out of it. I knew I should have just kept my mouth shut and waited for him to finish. But right at that moment, I also knew I had to do something. I couldn't let those poodles make the same mistake I had.

"Excuse me, ladies," I said. "But you'll want to have someone look over the contract before you sign it."

Ace turned and glared at me. "What do you think you're doing?" he snarled.

One of the poodles put her paw to her lips. She seemed to be deep in thought.

"We'd like to think about this, Ace," she said. "We'll get back to you."

"Wait a minute," he yelped. "I thought we had a deal."

The poodles smiled politely and scampered off.

Ace turned to us. His eyes were on fire. "You just cost me a big deal, kid. You better be prepared to add some bonus shows to your schedule to make up for it."

"Actually, I did want to talk to you about my performances," I said.

"What about them?" he growled.

I took a deep breath. "First of all, let me say that I appreciate everything you've done for me. I never really thought people might pay to hear my jokes. The schedule was crazy, but it forced me to come up with some great material. And what can I say about the dog treats? I have enough to last me for years." I paused and swallowed hard. "But I've decided to give up show business—at least, the part where we charge other dogs."

Ace raised his head and loomed over me. "You forget one thing, kid. I own you. You signed a twelve-month contract that automatically renews after a year. You can't quit until after the second year. So, you can just forget about all this silliness and get back to work."

"Not so fast," Marge said. "I'd like to see that contract."

"It's all perfectly legal," Ace said. "And your boy here signed it willingly."

Marge glared at him. "I said I want to see the contract."

"I can gladly get it for you, but it would take a few minutes," Ace said.

"Well, go and get it," Marge said. "We'll wait right here for you."

"As you wish," he said. Ace turned and sped away in the direction of the dog park.

We sat quietly and waited. Minutes later he returned with a paper between his teeth. He handed it to Marge.

"Read it for yourself, grandma."

Marge studied it for several minutes. Ace tapped his foot impatiently. I stared at the ground. Then I noticed a smile beginning to form on Marge's face.

"Rutherford," she said, "when's your birthday?"

"Next month," I answered.

"And how old will you be?"

"I'll be two…in people years, that is. I don't know how old that is in dog years."

Marge turned to Ace and held up the contract. "This is worthless," she said.

"What are you talking about?" he snapped.

"Rutherford is barely two years old. That's fourteen in dog years, making him a minor. And in this state, a minor cannot legally enter into a contract."

"You don't know what you're talking about!" Ace said.

"Oh, but I do," Marge said calmly. "Thanks to my previous owners, I know the laws in this state backward and forward."

Ace huffed. "Then I'll sue."

"Be my guest. But you couldn't win in a dog court or a people court. The law's the law. And minors are protected." She tossed the contract at his feet. "Come on, Rutherford. Your show-business career is over."

Ace growled, but it wasn't a vicious growl. It was as if he was upset with himself, not at us.

"He's booked for the next month. What am I supposed to do? Give back the deposits?"

Marge smiled. "That sounds like the wise thing to do."

Ace was angry, but he knew he had been licked. "Listen, I'll tell you what. If the kid's willing to do just one more job, I'll walk away and leave you alone—forever."

"Legally, he doesn't have to," Marge said.

"You mean after everything I did for the little guy, he can't do me one simple favor?"

"That's up to him."

I wasn't exactly sure what to do. I was thrilled that Marge had gotten me out of the contract, but I did feel bad for Ace. I wasn't sure why, exactly, but I did. I felt guilty about walking out on him even though he'd turned out to be kind of a creep. But what would it hurt to do one last show? It wouldn't kill me.

"What do you say?" Ace pleaded. "One final show, and you don't owe me a thing. If not, I may be inclined to sue, and even if you win, it's still gonna cost you a pretty penny in court costs."

I knew I could just walk away if I wanted to, but it sounded like Ace was prepared to make it as difficult as possible for me. Since I'm not the confrontational type, I decided to give him what he wanted and be done with it.

"Allright, Ace," I said. "One more show. But that's it."

"Are you sure?" Marge asked.

"I'm sure."

"Great," Ace said. "Let me go take care of the arrangements."

"By the way, when is this show?" I asked.

"Friday night," Ace said.

"Night?" All the other shows had been in the daytime. I had been able to slip away while Adam was at school. "Just how do you expect me to sneak out at night with everyone home?"

Ace rolled his eyes. "That's your problem, kid. Figure something out. Just be there."

"Where, exactly, is *there*?" Marge asked.

Ace didn't seem to appreciate all the questions. "It's not around here," he said. "It's near an industrial park on the other side of town. I'll give you the directions later."

"I don't like the sound of it," Marge said. "There aren't any homes over there."

"It's not your typical neighborhood," Ace snapped. "But, trust me, it's safe. Allright?"

"Trust *you*?" she said.

"Listen, I'm getting pretty tired of all of this." Ace pointed at me. "He agreed to do the show. So, why doesn't he just run along and think up some new material." He turned to leave. "And, oh, by the way, your stuff better be top-notch, kid. This is a pretty tough crowd." He promptly left before we could ask any more questions.

Once the Great Dane was out of earshot, Marge frowned and shook her head. "You don't have to do this show, you know. No matter what he tries to pull, we can win this battle in court."

"I know. But I'd just rather get it over with and not feel as though I owe him anything."

"It's your call," she said. "Hey, we'd better get home before we're missed."

We waved goodbye when we were back in our neighborhood and went our separate ways. I immediately began imagining a less-stressful life, without a performance every couple of days. I couldn't wait to finish up this last show and be done with it.

While I headed back, I found myself trying to think up a few new jokes, but as usual, nothing was coming. Whenever I'm under pressure to write a new stand-up routine, I struggle. I don't ever remember it being so tough when I was just telling jokes to friends for the fun of it.

I was almost home when I noticed another dog about a hundred yards away headed in my direction. Moments later, I could tell it was a bulldog, and he looked kind of familiar. It didn't take me long to figure out who it was.

"Jaws? Is that you?" I said.

He grinned. "Rutherford? I can't believe it. I didn't know you made it out. You got adopted? Really?"

I nodded.

"Well, that's just great."

"So, how's everything working out?" I asked. "You know…with your little problem?"

He shrugged. "Pretty good, I guess. Although I did chew up some Venetian blinds the other day. I got lonely. What can I say? But, other than that, it's been great."

"I'm so glad."

"By the way, are you still telling jokes?"

"Kind of. I made the mistake of hooking up with a Great Dane who offered to manage my career. He was booking stand-up jobs for me, but it got to be too much. And to tell you the truth, it just wasn't fun anymore."

"So, you're all done with him?"

"I have one more job, and then I'm out."

"Glad to hear. Hey, have you run into any of the old gang from the shelter?"

I grinned. "I see Marge all the time."

"No kidding. She always said she'd be in that shelter for the rest of her life. I'm really happy for her," he said. "And what about that little guy? The one who used to hide under his towel all the time?"

"Boomer."

"That's it. Boomer. Whatever happened to him?"

"Believe it or not, he got adopted, too," I said.

"Just goes to show you," Jaws said, "There's someone out there for everybody. Hey, you know what would be fun?

A little reunion. You, me, Marge, Boomer. What do you say?"

"I'd love it, but nobody knows where Boomer is."

"His new owner's not from around here?"

"To tell you the truth, I don't really know. But I do know that I didn't think much of the guy who adopted him. He was strange. It was almost as if he *wanted* a dog that was afraid of everything. It just didn't make sense."

"Hmmm, that *is* weird. Listen, I gotta go. Do me a favor—think about this little get-together idea."

"I will, but how will I find you?" I asked.

Jaws pointed to a row of houses across the street. "See the light-blue house with the black shutters? That's where I live. You can always find me there."

"That's easy enough," I said.

"Perfect. I'll see you real soon, I hope." He extended his paw, and we shook. "Take care, Rutherford. Hey, and it's nice to see you on four feet."

It was so great to see Jaws. He was a really nice guy. And if you took away that little chewing problem, he was, like, the perfect dog. It'd be fun to get together and reminisce.

As happy as I was to see Jaws, though, it made me just as sad to think about Boomer. I had no idea where he was or how to find him. And although I hated even thinking it, I didn't know if he was alive or dead. I could only hope he was okay.

One thing was certain—if I spent any more time worrying about him, I'd get really depressed and I'd never be able to think up new jokes.

But no matter how hard I tried, I couldn't get him out of my head. There were a lot of happy stories of dogs being adopted and living happily ever after, but in Boomer's case, it was a story without an ending.

Chapter 14

The Final Stage

I stretched out on Adam's bed as he scratched behind my ears. It was heaven. I could have stayed there all day. But there was no time. I had a job to do.

I needed to come up with one more routine. After that, I could entertain friends whenever I wanted to instead of when Ace told me I had to.

I sat up and jumped off the bed. I went into the living room and plopped down onto a pillow the family had gotten just for me. Actually, they'd bought three of them —one for Adam's room, one for the kitchen, and this one. They'd even had my name embroidered on all of them. It was now time to put my thinking cap on and get to work.

I remembered Ace saying something about this last audience being a tough group, so I knew my material had to be A+. I began thinking of situations a typical dog might find themselves in, and then I looked for a funny twist of some kind.

I took my paws and pressed them against the sides of my head as hard as I could. I would make this happen. I would force my brain to come up with quality jokes that would entertain even the pickiest audience.

Ten minutes later, all I had managed to do was give myself a massive headache.

I knew I shouldn't try to force myself. I knew ideas were more likely to pop into my head when I wasn't even trying. It was funny how that worked. I put my head down on the pillow, and...

Twenty minutes later, I was awakened by a shrill sound—the *vroom* of the vacuum cleaner. Since I had been dreaming about the night Horace abandoned me, I was more than happy to rejoin the living.

"Oh, I'm sorry," Mrs. Sampson said. "I didn't mean to scare you." She crouched down and stroked the top of my head. "You don't have to get up. I'll vacuum around you."

It was nice of her to offer, but there was no way I was going to let that monster (the vacuum, not Adam's mom) dance around me with those shrill, ear-piercing sounds. I made a hasty exit.

"I'm sorry, Rutherford," she said as I scampered down the hallway.

I desperately needed a writer's retreat—someplace that would encourage the necessary spark. I tried to think of the ideal spot, but none immediately came to mind. I finally decided maybe Mother Nature would provide.

I headed into the kitchen, squeezed through the doggy door, and found a soft spot in some high grass on the side of the garage. I closed my eyes, took several deep breaths, and waited for inspiration to strike.

When I emerged from my trance some thirty minutes later, I realized I had done it. I had put together a winning routine. It wasn't the best stuff I had ever come up with, but I was hopeful it would be good enough to accomplish two things—entertain a demanding crowd, and get Ace off my back, permanently.

I went behind the garage and rehearsed the new material. I imagined the response from the crowd. It's critical for me, or any comedian, to get the timing down. Timing is everything when it comes to joke-telling.

🐾 🐾 🐾

I counted the days until my last show. I wanted it to be over and done with, but at the same time, I had an image to uphold. It had to be good. After all, I was Rutherford, Canine Comic. As much as I wanted to put it behind me, a halfhearted effort was simply unacceptable. I had learned that you want to leave the crowd satisfied but hungry for more—just not so hungry they insisted on having more right then and there.

I met up with Marge the next day—I'd decided to bounce the routine off of her. She was always a good test audience.

She listened as I moved from one joke to the next. I made it a point to pay attention to her reactions to each joke. I could tell which ones were a hit. The ones that only generated a weak smile, at best, I would have to consider either revising or just getting rid of completely.

When I was finished, like a true friend, Marge stood and banged her paws on the ground--her way of applauding.

"Bravo!" she said.

I bowed. The one thing about Marge I really like is that she isn't afraid to tell me if my material is weak. And she always manages to do it in a nice way. That made it easy to take.

"It sounds like you're going to go out with a bang," she said. "I can't imagine any audience, even a tough crowd, not loving that material."

"You really think so?"

"Absolutely," she said. "Now, refresh my memory. When's the show, again?"

"Tomorrow night."

"What time?"

I didn't want to tell her. I knew how she worried.

"Eleven o'clock," I said without looking at her.

She shook her head. "Rutherford, you know how I feel about this. I'm not going to try to stop you from doing it, but you'd better be careful."

"I will. Don't worry."

"I just don't understand why it's so late." She began pacing. "All the dogs I know are fast asleep at that time."

"I know. I know. I'll be fine. And it's the last one. Then Ace'll be out of my hair forever."

"Just promise me one thing," she said. "If something doesn't smell right, you hightail it out of there as fast as you can. Agreed?"

I didn't want to admit it to her, but I was a little nervous myself. I didn't like not knowing who the audience was. Why all the mystery? I wasn't crazy about traveling so far from home. And I sure wasn't a fan of such a late show.

But I had given my word, so I would just have to make the best of it.

I spent most of the next day rehearsing and refining my routine. When Adam got home from school, I decided to take a well-deserved break. We threw a ball around in the back yard, and then we took a walk. At dinnertime, I was almost too nervous to eat, but I forced myself to finish the entire bowl.

I needed to make everything seem as normal as possible. I couldn't have anyone thinking I was sick or something, and watching me more closely. The plan was to meet up with Ace at the dog park at ten-thirty. It would take us most of a half -hour to get to where we were going.

At nine-thirty, I followed Adam into his room for bed. Fifteen minutes later, he had drifted off. I kept my eyes on his parents. Since I always slept in Adam's room, they would just assume I was with him when they went to bed—at least, I hoped so.

Trying to sneak out on a Friday night complicated things. Mr. and Mrs. Sampson would be up past the exact moment I needed to make my exit. For all of this to work, two things had to happen—they couldn't hear me sneak out, and they couldn't notice I was gone.

At 10:14, I poked my head into the hallway. Adam's dad had fallen asleep on the couch, but his mom seemed wide awake watching television. I decided to take advantage of the fact that the TV audio was nice and loud. It would provide good cover for my escape.

I made my move—down the hallway, into the kitchen, and through the doggie door. I waited a minute just to make certain I had gotten away. When I heard nothing, I headed in the direction of the dog park.

It was a relatively quiet night. An occasional car would drive by, but I didn't encounter anyone—human or canine—taking a late-night walk. The moon was nearly full. It helped light the path for me, but I would have been just fine. As a member of the hound family, I'm blessed with an above-average snout.

It was just after ten-thirty when I met up with Ace at the dog park.

"You're late," he said.

"It's not easy to sneak out at this time of night. I had to make sure no one saw me."

"Whatever. Let's go."

Ace didn't appear to be in the best of moods. I guess I couldn't blame him. He was about to lose his golden goose. I wasn't really sure what that meant. Marge had used it one time to describe me.

I followed Ace along the south end of the park into a residential area. I noticed at least one light on in most of the houses we passed, and most had their porch lights on. If you added in the glow from streetlights, it made me feel fairly safe. This was the latest I could remember ever being out if you didn't count the night Horace dumped me in the woods.

About twenty minutes later, we left the safety of that quiet neighborhood and entered what appeared to be an industrial park. There weren't any homes, just a string of one- and two-story buildings that all looked the same, with big parking lots—loads of big parking lots.

We continued for about ten or so minutes when we came upon an area that was surrounded by an eight-foot-tall chain-link fence with three strands of barbed wire at the top. It was an eerie-looking place, to say the least. We followed the fence around the property for a couple hundred yards until Ace stopped and began looking for something.

"Over here," a voice called out.

In the distance, I could see a large dog in the shadows on the other side of the fence. As we got closer, I became more frightened. This dog was one scary-looking dude. Half of his left ear was missing, and he was limping. He appeared to be a member of the pitbull family. If I had to guess, I'd say he was an American pit bull terrier, but I wasn't positive.

"Where's the gate?" Ace asked.

"It's about a quarter-mile that way," the pitbull said, pointing north. "But it's locked."

"Then how are we supposed to get in?"

"Over here."

We followed our host to a spot about thirty feet away. He was standing next to a hole that had been dug under the fence.

"Right this way," he said. "But keep it to yourself. The bosses don't know anything about it."

"Mum's the word," Ace said as he slithered under the fence. I followed him.

"You got a name?" Ace asked the pit.

"Sledge Hammer. But you can call me Sledge."

"So, where are we headed…Sledge?" Ace asked.

Sledge pointed across the fenced-in area. "Way over there. Away from everything."

He led us over some rough ground for the next several minutes. Soon, I could make out the sound of barking. Loud barking. Mean barking. It made me nervous.

"What *is* this place?" I whispered to Ace. He could probably hear the uneasiness in my voice.

"Relax, kid," he answered. "Just put on a killer show and don't worry about it."

We followed Sledge to a rundown section of the property. Trash everywhere. Buildings with peeling paint, broken windows, and dangling gutters. He took us to a room with a dirt floor. It had a section that had been roped off. It almost looked like a boxing ring.

"Here's your stage, pal," Sledge said. "The audience will fill in around the ropes there."

"Okay," I said, my voice cracking.

"You two can wait here while I go round up the troops," he said. "Ace says you're a real funny guy. Let's hope so. We could use a good laugh. There aren't too many smiles around this place." He turned to leave. "I'll be right back."

We watched Sledge until he disappeared down a hallway. I took a good look at the surroundings. Something wasn't right about this place.

"Ace, where are we, exactly? I didn't see any signs or anything. And what did Sledge mean by 'there aren't too many smiles around here'?"

"Kid, you ask too many questions. In a minute, this room'll be filled with some pretty tough characters, and they'll be expecting a killer show. You *don't* want to disappoint them. So, why don't you just rehearse your material and relax."

I forced a smile. I had no idea what was to come. I could only hope it would be quick and painless.

Chapter 15

An Encore Performance

I ducked under the rope into the stage area. Since the crowd would be on all sides, I would have to keep moving to keep eye contact with all of them. I closed my eyes and went over each of the jokes I would be telling.

After about ten minutes, Sledge reappeared. This time he wasn't alone. Filing past him and muscling each other for front-row seats was one of the scariest-looking audiences I had ever seen. It was the first time I could remember a crowd made up of all the same breed—pitbulls At least twenty to thirty of them.

I used to be a little uncomfortable around these dogs, but while I was at the shelter, I met a couple of them, and they had turned out to be just regular dogs. I didn't want to assume this bunch were all as edgy and mean as they looked. I had to believe the ugly surroundings had something to do with how scared I felt..

Ace joined me on the stage. "You ready, kid?"

I swallowed hard and nodded.

"Okay, let's do this." He stood on his hind legs and waved his front paws to get everyone's attention. "Guys, quiet down, please." He waited for them to settle. "As promised, I've got a real treat for you. I discovered this act in a local dog park, and he's come a long way since then. So, if you're quite ready, let's hear it for Rutherford, Canine Comic."

Grunts, snarls, barking, and howling followed as the houselights dimmed and a spotlight filled the center of the stage. It was showtime.

I smiled confidently and swiveled slowly in a full circle to see all of the audience. There was only one word to describe this bunch—*weird*.

Many of them looked like Sledge—either chewed up or with parts missing. Some looked as though they had been through a war. A few were even bandaged up.

Then, just as I was about to deliver my opening joke, I spotted a group of dogs in the far corner of the room. They weren't pitbulls. There were about fifteen of them, and they were every breed imaginable. They were all pretty small —probably no more than twenty pounds each.

And then I noticed something unusual about them. They were all standing still, but for some reason, they seemed to be moving from side to side. When I looked more closely, I could see they were all shaking.

But why? They couldn't have been cold. It was warm in this place—too warm, actually. What was their problem?

Ace stuck his head through the ropes on one side of the ring. "Let's go! Let's go! What are you waiting for?"

I could hear some rumbling in the crowd. It was time to get to work. The mystery of the little dogs would have to wait, for the time being.

I took a deep breath and jumped in.

"Good evening, everyone. It's so nice to be here…wherever *here* is." I glanced at Ace, who was standing offstage. That jab was for him, but he pretended not to notice. "Now, get this. I was at an internet café the other day, and I noticed a Labrador and a Dalmatian having a conversation.

"The Dalmatian said, 'Hey, you should check out my website.' The Labrador asked where he could find it, and the Dalmatian said, 'Just go to www.dalmation-dot-dot-dot-dot-dot-dot-dot-dot.'"

I heard a few chuckles but nothing overwhelming. I guess there weren't any computer geeks in the crowd.

"Speaking of Dalmatians," I said, "did you hear about the Dalmatian who wolfed down this huge meal and then said, 'Boy, now, that really hit the spots.'" Again there was little to no response. "Get it? Spots?"

A couple of dogs in the front row smiled.

It was right about then I realized this was not a roomful of geniuses. They didn't seem to appreciate or understand a basic play on words. I would need to dumb down the material if I wanted to get through to them.

"Hey, here's a question for you. How do you get a dog to stop barking in the back seat of the car?" I paused. "It's pretty simple—put him in the front seat." A few chuckles followed. That was good.

"Did you hear about the dog owner who thought his dog was a whiz at math? Whenever he asked the dog what six minus six was, the dog said nothing."

It took the gang a few seconds to get it, but now the room was starting to buzz.

"Hey, what's the difference between Santa Claus and a warm dog?" I looked around as if waiting for an answer. "Well, Santa wears a whole suit, a dog just pants!"

Ace let out a roar, and that seemed to trigger a response from the others.

"By the way, does anyone out there know how to make a dog float?" I waited to see if there were any takers. When it was clear they were all stumped, I delivered the punch line: "All you need is root beer, two scoops of ice cream, and one scoop of dog."

Unlike the reaction for the other jokes, the applause meter registered big time with that one. I continued with several more one-liners—each a bit funnier than the last. About halfway through the show, I shared one of my favorites.

"This man was walking down the street when he heard a voice say, 'Pssst, come over here!' The man looked around, but all he could see was this mangy old greyhound. 'I'm talking to you,' the greyhound said. The man couldn't believe his eyes.

"'Listen,' the dog said, 'you gotta help me get loose.' The man could see that the dog was tied to a parking meter. 'I gotta get back to the track. I'm a famous racer. I don't belong here. Would you believe I've won more than thirty races in my career?'

"The man was beside himself. He couldn't believe he had stumbled on a talking dog. *This could make me a millionaire*, he thought. *I can see it now—nightclubs, TV talk shows, movies. I'll be rich. But first I gotta find this dog's owner and see if he's for sale.*

"A minute or so later, this old lady walked up. 'Excuse me, ma'am, is this your dog?' The old lady nodded. 'Is he, by any chance, for sale?' the man asked. The old woman seemed confused. 'You don't want to buy this mangy old thing.' 'But I do,' the man insisted. 'I'll tell you what. I'll give you a thousand dollars for him right here and now.'

"The woman thought he was crazy, but she couldn't pass up good money. 'Okay,' she said, 'but I think you're making a big mistake.'

"The man pulled the money from his wallet and handed it over. 'This dog is amazing,' he said. 'I don't know why you were willing to part with him.'

"'I'll tell you why,' she said, 'because he's a big fat liar. He never won a single race in his life.'"

I paused, waiting for applause. At least, I hoped it would come. And although it took a few extra seconds for this group to process things, they were soon in stitches. It was official. I was a hit.

I looked offstage and noticed a big smile on Ace's face. I had a feeling he would have a hard time letting me go after this, but he had no choice.

I hate to admit this, but when I first laid eyes on this crowd, I considered laying the proverbial egg—doing a terrible show with lame jokes just so Ace would be happy to see me move on. But I couldn't. I couldn't disappoint an audience. I guess it was the pure entertainer in me that refused to surrender. I had to perform at the highest possible level every time I went out on stage.

For the next fifteen minutes, I delivered some of my best stuff—*primo* material, if I do say so myself. And I think it was safe to say I had won over my audience. They were eating out of my paw.

Then I began to notice something strange with all the little dogs sitting in the corner. After each joke, I would glance in their direction, and none of them laughed or even smiled.

Either they didn't get the jokes, or they didn't find them funny. Talk about a tough crowd.

I went on for a few more minutes, and then it was time for my finale. This would be the last joke I would ever tell to paying customers, so it had to be good.

"Let me leave you with this one, fellows. It's a story about a human named Ernie who was all excited, and a little nervous, about meeting his blind date. She lived on the thirty-fifth floor of a high-rise apartment building.

"So, he gets off the elevator, walks down the hallway, and knocks on her door. When she opens it, Ernie couldn't be happier. She's gorgeous. 'Won't you come in,' she says. He follows her into the living room.

"'I'll be ready in a few minutes,' she tells him. 'Why don't you play with my dog while you're waiting. His name is Bandit. He loves everyone, and he's really smart. He rolls over, shakes hands, sits up, and if you make a hoop with your arms, he'll jump right through.'

"Ernie walks out onto the balcony while his date gets ready for their big evening. The dog follows him out to the balcony and immediately starts doing tricks. He rolls over, sits up, and shakes hands. Ernie is quite impressed. He makes a hoop with his arms to see if Bandit will jump through. And, as promised, the dog jumps right through his arms…and right off the balcony…thirty-five floors up.

"When Ernie's date joins him, she says, "So, isn't Bandit just the smartest and happiest dog you've ever seen?' Ernie thinks for a minute and says, 'To tell the truth, he seemed a little depressed to me.'"

Rim shot, courtesy of Ace, followed by thunderous applause.

Ace ran onto the stage.

"So, what'd I tell you? Isn't he great?"

More cheers. Some of the pits in the front row started chanting, "Rutherford, Rutherford, Rutherford…"

"When's he comin' back?" one of them yelled.

Ace turned to me and shrugged. "What do you say?"

Wait just a minute. What was he doing? He knew this was my last performance. He knew the contract was worthless. Nothing like applying a little pressure.

"Rutherford, Rutherford, Rutherford…" The pitbulls were going crazy. They wanted an immediate answer.

I didn't want to say *yes* to a return engagement, but if I said *no*, I wasn't sure if I'd live to tell about it. There seemed to be only one thing to do.

"Okay," I said. "I'll come back in a week."

A roar went up. The chanting got louder. Some of the dogs were now climbing into the ring. Even Ace looked a little concerned.

"Time to go," he said.

I followed him off the stage and through the crowd. A few of the dogs patted me on the back. They may have been meant to be friendly taps, but these guys didn't know their own strength.

In order to exit, we needed to pass right by the little dogs. As we got closer, my heart started racing. I stopped short. I couldn't believe my eyes. There, in the middle, was Boomer. I was sure it was him.

"Boomer, is that you? It's me, Rutherford."

Boomer lowered his head. Some of the other dogs began staring at us.

"Boomer?"

He looked up. "Don't talk to me. I'll get in trouble. Just leave me alone and go." He turned and ran to the back of the group.

Ace grabbed me by the back of the neck. "C'mon." He pulled me out of the room. We ran down a long hallway and exited the building into the darkness.

"Who were you talking to back there?" he said.

"A friend of mine. His name is Boomer. I knew him back at the shelter."

"Don't make a habit of it," Ace said. "Now, let's get out of here."

I refused to budge. "I'm not moving until I know what's going on. What is this place, anyway? What's wrong with those little dogs? And why did you tell them I'd be back. I'm not coming back."

"I just thought you'd want to help out your fellow dog. But if you'd rather be selfish, and refuse to assist the downtrodden, then I guess you don't have to."

What was he talking about? The downtrodden? I was still completely confused.

"You didn't answer my questions," I said. I was getting angry.

"I didn't tell you who these dogs were because I didn't want you feeling sorry for them. They just want to be treated like every other dog. If I had told you about some of the lives they've led, you would have treated them differently. They don't want your pity. They just want to be able to laugh again."

"I still don't get it."

"Allright," Ace said. "Cards on the table. This place is a rehab center."

"A what?"

"A rehab center. A place where dogs come to heal... to get better...to get away from abusive owners. Did you see the condition of some of those dogs? They've led pretty rough lives, to say the least. They come here to get fixed up physically and emotionally."

It was starting to make sense. A lot of those dogs *were* in pretty bad shape. And no one had to tell me about abusive owners. Horace was right up there at the top of the list.

"What about those little dogs?" I asked. "The ones in the back who were shaking the entire time."

"Those are the ones with serious emotional issues. The program here will help them deal with their problems, and when they're all better, they'll be placed in loving homes."

"That friend of mine I was talking to…he's afraid of everything."

"See. That's what I've been trying to tell you. Your friend will get all the care he needs right here." Ace tilted his head and smiled. "So, won't you consider coming again? After everything these dogs have been through, would it be right to deny them a few laughs?"

I knew what it was like to be abandoned and left for dead. How could I turn my back on these needy souls? It was the least I could do. What would it hurt to do one more show before parting ways with Ace?

"Okay," I said. "One more show."

Ace grinned. "I knew you'd do the right thing."

Just then Sledge came outside. He was leading all of the little dogs somewhere. I'm not quite sure why, but for some odd reason, I felt this urge to follow them. I wanted to see where Boomer was going.

"Let's go," Ace said.

I pointed at Sledge. "I want to know where he's taking them."

"What do you care?"

"I just want to see."

"I don't recommend it," Ace said.

"Well, I'm not leaving here until I know where he's taking Boomer."

Ace rolled his eyes and grunted. "Allright, allright. But let's be discreet. We don't want them thinking we're spying on them or anything."

Ace and I followed Sledge and the others across the compound to a distant part of the property where there was a large cage. Sledge pointed to a hole that had been dug under one side of it. All of the little dogs jumped into the hole, scurried under the fence, and popped up on the other side.

Sledge looked back in the direction of the building where the show had been, as if he was waiting for something. A minute or so later, ten other pitbulls ran to join him.

Next to the open hole was a huge boulder. The pits got on one side of it, and with all their might, they managed to slide it over the open hole, which made it impossible for the little dogs to escape.

"It's like they're prisoners," I whispered to Ace.

"They're not prisoners, they're patients. It's for their own good. It's to protect them. You wouldn't want them getting loose and running all over by themselves. They could get hurt. They could get hit by a car. Trust me, it's the best thing."

"Okay, I guess you're right," I said reluctantly. But it still bothered me to see those helpless little dogs all caged up like that.

"By the way" Ace said, "do you think you could find your way back to this place next week by yourself? I've got a meeting with a potential client right before that. There's this Irish setter who can sing the National Anthem while gargling. He could be very big. I gotta sign him." He grinned. "So, I'll meet you here next Friday at the same time, right?

I nodded.

We eventually found our way to the spot where we had first entered. Ace scooted under the fence, and I followed. As I made my way back home, I kept thinking of Boomer. I wasn't crazy about his living conditions, but I was happy to see he was at least getting help. I couldn't wait to see him in the weeks and months to come once he was well enough to leave that place, find a new home with loving owners, and start his new life. He sure deserved it.

Chapter 16
Operation Boomer

I managed to make it back home without being missed. I squeezed through the doggie door, scooted across the kitchen floor, down the hallway, and into Adam's room. He was still sound asleep. I was looking forward to joining him in a little peaceful slumber for the next few hours.

I was exhausted. I hopped up onto my pillow and tried to doze off, but I kept thinking about Boomer. I was looking forward to seeing him in a week; hopefully, I would get a chance to talk to him next time. He had seemed reluctant to chat tonight. Maybe it was all part of the therapy he was receiving. No outside contact, I guessed.

Next morning, I joined Mr. Sampson on a three-mile run. It was good to stretch out the old legs. It also helped me maintain my weight. Basset hounds, because of how we're put together, tend to put on weight pretty easily. All of the calories seemed to go right to our mid-sections, which in turn puts more strain on our joints.

It was Saturday—and that always meant a trip to the dog park. I couldn't wait to see Marge to tell her about bumping into Boomer. She'd be happy to hear he was getting help with his fear problem.

I waited patiently in the driveway for Adam and his dad to finish lunch. The drive to the dog park only took a few minutes. When we arrived, I jumped up onto the middle seat and stuck my head out the window. I could hear a ton of barking, but it was friendly barking. In no time, we had parked the van, and I was off-leash and on my own. It was a great feeling.

I immediately looked for Marge. I found her with some of the others in mid-conversation, updating each other on the previous week's activities.

"Marge!" I yelled as I ran in her direction.

She trotted over to meet me. We immediately hugged.

"Well, how does it feel?" she said. "How does it feel to be out from under that contract?"

"Good," I said. I wasn't sure how I was going to tell her I still had one more performance to do.

"So, how did it go last night?"

"It was a different kind of crowd, but they really seemed to like my stuff."

"I'm glad to hear that," she said. "Now you can just relax and tell funny stories whenever *you* want to, not when Ace tells you to."

"Yeah, that'll be great," I said. "Hey, you'll never believe who I saw last night."

"Who?"

"Boomer."

"Boomer?! You're kidding? How's he doing? Is he happy with his new owner?"

"Well, it's kind of a long story," I said.

Marge smiled. "Like I told you once before, at my age it's best to keep things short and sweet. How about the condensed version?"

I laughed. "I'm not sure whatever happened with the man who adopted him. All I know is that he's getting the help he needs."

"What do you mean?"

"He's at a rehab center. They'll help him get over his nervousness. And then they'll find him a good home."

Marge scratched her head. "A rehab center for *dogs*? Around here? I've never heard of that before. Are you sure?"

"Yeah, I saw it myself."

"What, exactly, did you see?"

"Ace took me to this place. It's pretty far away, and there aren't any houses. There were all these dogs. Pit-bulls, mostly."

"Pitbulls?"

"Uh-huh. Most of them were in bad shape. They were all beat up. Some had nicked-up ears and tails. And a lot of them were bruised. Let me tell you, it wasn't pretty."

Marge suddenly had this skeptical look on her face. "What else did you see?"

"Besides the pitbulls, there was a bunch of little dogs. That's where I saw Boomer. And they were messed up, too. They were all shaking. But don't worry, they're gonna get help."

Marge's expression had turned to anger. "What else?"

"Umm. Well, they had a weird stage. It kind of looked like a boxing ring. And all the dogs stayed on the other side of the ropes."

Marge began pacing. She seemed disturbed by the things I'd told her.

"What's wrong? I don't understand."

"Rutherford, that was no rehab center. That was a dog-fighting operation."

"Dog fighting?"

"Yes. That's exactly what it was."

I was confused. "But that doesn't make any sense. Boomer's no fighter. Why would he be there?"

Marge stared at the ground and shook her head. She was silent. It was almost as if she didn't want to answer the question.

"What's wrong? Tell me," I said.

She took a long breath. "You understand what happens at one of those places, right?"

"Not exactly."

"Well, I guess you're old enough to know," she said as she sat down next to me. "There are people out there—bad people—who enjoy watching two dogs fight one another—to the death sometimes. So, they breed dogs—usually pitbulls—to be fighters. Then they charge other people to come watch them. And they bet on which dog will win."

"But why?" I asked. "Why would you pay to see dogs hurt each other? I don't get it."

"Why do people stop and stare at accidents on the highway?" she said. "It's human nature, I guess."

I found myself getting upset. "But it's not dog nature. We don't do those things."

Marge stroked my head with her paw. "I can't explain it, Rutherford. I wish I could."

"So, do the little dogs fight each other, too?"

"No, I'm afraid not. The little, timid ones are what they call *bait dogs*. They're tossed into the ring so the fighting dogs will have something to practice on."

Wait a minute. That didn't make any sense. "But those little guys wouldn't stand a chance," I said.

"You're right. And most of them don't survive."

I could barely get the words out. "Is that what's going to happen to Boomer?"

"It's unlikely we'll ever see him again. I'm sorry to have to tell you that."

I felt myself about to erupt. "Then we have to do something. We have to stop this. We have to save him."

"Rutherford, get serious. Look at us. What chance would we have against all those fighting dogs?"

I looked out at all of the other dogs in the park. "It's not just you and me. Look around this place. We have a small army here. If we can convince the others to join us, we might just be able to pull it off."

"And you really think you'll be able to convince these pets to do battle with professional fighters? It's not going to happen."

I thought for a minute. Maybe there was another way. Maybe there was a way to rescue Boomer without having to battle the pitbulls.

"What if I came up with an escape plan that helped us save Boomer, but one where we wouldn't have to fight anybody? We'd just break him out of there. That could work, right?

"Unless you can guarantee no one will get hurt, I'm not sure you'll get any volunteers."

"But, Marge—"

She placed her paw on my snout. "Rutherford, you can't ask these dogs to risk their lives to save Boomer. Most of them don't even know him."

"But we can't just do nothing." This was all so frustrating. "I'll think of something. I have to. And when I go back there next Friday night for my final performance, I guarantee that I won't be alone."

"Wait a minute," she said. "I thought you already did your last show."

"That's what I thought, too. But when Ace told me that place was a rehab center, and that I couldn't turn my back on these poor helpless dogs who were being nursed back to health, I agreed to do one more show."

She shook her head. "No way. Either you tell him you're through, or I will."

"I can't do that, Marge. Don't you see? It's the only way we can get back in there to save Boomer."

"Listen, I love Boomer as much as you do," she said. "But you have no idea what you're getting yourself into. You're going to be killed, pure and simple."

I turned and noticed someone walking toward us. It was the older lady who had adopted Marge."

"Time to go, girl," she said. "We have company tonight." She attached the end of a leash to Marge's collar. As they passed me, Marge leaned in my direction.

"To be continued," she whispered. "Just don't do anything stupid until we talk."

As I sat alone in the middle of the dog park, I found myself trying to come up with a way of springing Boomer from that prison without anyone, human or canine, ever finding out. It was going to be a real challenge.

⁂

When we got back home, I wasn't interested in playing or eating or anything. I wouldn't be happy until I had figured out a way to save Boomer. I needed to come up with a foolproof strategy that would buy Boomer his freedom without getting anyone else hurt. I wouldn't be able to live with myself if anything happened to him, and I hadn't done everything in my power to help.

I kept thinking about all of the dogs at the dog park. Surely, they would step up and help out one of their own. We dogs had always stuck together in the past. Why not now?

But what if Marge was right? What if none of them wanted to stick their necks out? Then what? But I don't suppose I could blame them if they refused. This promised to be dangerous. Dogs could get hurt—or worse.

I soon realized that I was overthinking all of this. Why worry about something that might never happen? I needed to get my butt back to that dog park and do my best to recruit a first-class posse. Who knows? Maybe they'd surprise Marge and do the right thing.

Heck, if we showed up with an army of twenty or thirty, I doubted if those pitbulls would want to tangle with us. Some of the regulars at the park—Labs and goldens and German shepherds—were pretty good size. It's not as if we'd be showing up with a platoon of toy poodles or anything. Some of our crew could look pretty intimidating if they wanted to.

And that was the key—*if* they wanted to.

For the rest of the day and late into the night, I tried to think of a way to get Boomer out of that cage and then off the property. No matter what scenario I drew up in my head, nothing seemed good enough to withstand an attack from those pitbulls.

I thought long and hard until my head ached. Before I knew it, I had fallen asleep.

And then, just like that, the sun was up, and it was morning again. Adam and his parents were getting ready to go to church. They'd be gone for close to two hours. It was always nice to have the house to myself. It would give me time to work on a battle plan.

But wait a minute. What was I doing? I shouldn't be wasting precious time wracking my brain. With the family gone, I could easily sneak out of the house and head to the dog park. Yeah, that was it. I needed to enlist a few recruits for a dangerous but noble undertaking.

I decided to wait by the back door while everyone was getting ready.

"Why are you standing there?" Mrs. Sampson said.

Oh, no, I was too obvious. The last thing I needed was for them to think I was waiting to bolt the minute they left. I had to busy myself with other things.

I strolled over to my food dish and scarfed down a few mouthfuls. I wasn't hungry, but I needed to act normal.

"Adam, we're about to leave," Mr. Sampson yelled from the living room.

I hopped onto my bed near the back door and pretended I had fallen asleep. A minute later, I heard Adam's wheelchair glide into the kitchen. He stopped next to me, bent over, and began stroking the top of my head. I always loved it when he did that. I immediately opened my eyes and licked his hand.

Mr. Sampson poked his head into the room. "Come on, guy, we're gonna be late."

"Okay, Dad, one minute." Adam waited for his dad to leave. He wheeled over to the refrigerator, opened the door, and pulled out a small plastic bag with leftover bacon from breakfast. He fished in it for one of the strips, broke it in half, and handed it to me. I still wasn't hungry, but let me make one thing perfectly clear. When it comes to bacon, hungry or not, we dogs are all in. I scarfed it down in one gulp.

Adam laughed. "Just the bacon, not my fingers, buddy."

I continued licking his hand until he pulled it away.

"Now you be a good boy, you hear? We'll be back about noon."

I waited until I heard the front door close before getting up. I made my way into the living room, lifted my front paws onto the windowsill, and watched as they drove off.

I sprinted back into the kitchen and slipped through the doggie door. Operation Boomer had officially begun.

Chapter 17
Mission Improbable

I made it to the dog park in less than twenty minutes. I scanned the entire area. Since we usually came here on Saturdays, there were a lot of unfamiliar faces. This was going to make it a lot tougher.

But what could I do? A life hung in the balance. I would just need to plead my case and hope to convince at least some of these dogs to join the quest.

I walked to the center of the park and began barking as loudly as my lungs would allow. It wasn't a friendly bark, It was the kind of bark a dog in peril would make. It got the attention I was hoping for. Within seconds, I was surrounded.

"What's going on?" a fox terrier asked.

"Are you okay?" a pug said.

"*I'm* fine," I said, "but there's some of our own out there who's not okay."

"What are you talking about?" an Airedale shouted out.

I decided it would be best to lay things out in order. I didn't want to leave out a single detail. I took my time, telling my story from my days at the breeding farm until now. I told them about Horace...and the coyotes...and the fellow who hit me on the highway...and the vet clinic...and Vickie...and Marge...and Boomer...and Adam's family...and Ace...and stand-up gigs.

I ended with the dog-fighting operation. I wanted to build the suspense. For this to work, they needed to see the journey I had taken, and the obstacles I had overcome. Then and only then would I be able to inspire them to join me on this very dangerous, but hopefully rewarding, mission.

"You want us to tangle with a bunch of pitbulls?" a Samoyed said.

"Are you out of your mind?" a greyhound added.

I sat back and held up my front paws. "If we do this thing right, it'll just be a rescue operation. We won't even have to see the big dogs."

"How can you be so sure of that?" the Samoyed said.

"I've got a plan," I said, "a foolproof plan to get us in and out—no problem." Of course, I didn't have any plan. I was just hoping that, between now and next Friday, I would come up with something.

A pug worked her way to the front row. "I want to hear this so-called *foolproof* plan."

"Right now?" I said.

The pug looked at me skeptically. It appeared she was prepared to call my bluff. "Right now."

"You know, I'd like to, guys, but I'm afraid it'd take too long to list all of the details. This plan has a lot of angles."

The pug sat and snorted. "If you expect any of us to risk our necks to save this Boomer none of us knows, then the least you can do is tell us your plan."

It made no sense to continue. I needed to come clean.

"Okay, I haven't actually come up with a plan yet. I'm sorry I misled you. It's just that the sweetest, nicest dog you'd ever want to meet is about to become lunch for a bunch of mongrels. And we're the only chance he has." There. I had spilled my guts. I had nothing more to say. They were either in or out.

A yellow Lab who had been standing in the back moved to the front. "Hey, I know you. Aren't you the comedian? Don't you put on shows around here?"

"Guilty as charged," I said.

"Then let me give you a little piece of advice. Maybe you just tell your jokes and not get mixed up in stuff like this. You'll live longer."

I didn't know what to say. I decided to ignore the advice and just move on. This wasn't about me.

"Isn't there anyone here who's willing to lend a paw?" I asked.

"Listen, fellow," the greyhound said, "nothing personal, but I can't agree to something this dangerous with so little information. If you do come up with a foolproof plan —and I mean *guaranteed foolproof*—then, and only then, will I consider it."

Some of the other dogs chimed in with similar comments. By the end of our conversation, I knew what I needed to do. I had to present them with a surefire rescue plan —and if they were comfortable with it, they *might* be willing to help. If not, then I was on my own.

I appreciated that they had left the door open, but how could I promise them in no uncertain terms we would all return without a scrape and with Boomer in paw? I couldn't do that. I suppose I was asking for too much. I'd hoped they would offer to help, regardless of the risks. It wasn't practical, and I now realized that. It was up to me.

I spent the next few days trying to figure out a way to save Boomer. I'm no fighter. And I couldn't count on just snatching him from under their noses and hope to get away on foot. I could keep up with Mr. Sampson when he went on a jog, but I could never outrun a trained fighting dog. It seemed pretty hopeless.

But first things first. I needed to think up some new jokes for the routine. I was hoping that while my creative juices were stewing, I would also come up with a way to rescue my friend.

🐾 🐾 🐾

I was sitting on the kitchen floor at Adam's feet during dinner on Friday night. An entire week had passed, and I still hadn't come up with an idea. I had managed to put together a comedy routine for tonight's performance, but that was it. I'd just have to improvise when I got there and hope for a chance to make a move. I was disappointed with myself.

Mrs. Sampson set a bowl of mashed potatoes on the table. "Did I tell you about the call I got today from the neighbors?" she said to her husband.

"Which one?" Adam's dad asked.

"Sally next door. She called to see if our cable TV was out."

"Was it?" Adam said.

"No," she answered. "Everything was fine. It turns out that something—probably a squirrel—chewed right through the cable where it goes into their house. And they even had it wrapped in heavy metallic tape."

"That's what I call a pretty good set of incisors," Mr. Sampson said.

"We should probably check our cable sometime," she said.

And right at that moment—at that precise second—the light bulb went on, and I knew exactly how I could save Boomer. It was the perfect solution. And it was foolproof.

For the next couple of hours, I drew a map of the dog-fighting place in my head from memory. I pictured the hole under the fence where we had entered the property, the location of the room where I had done my stand-up routine, the exact spot where all of the little dogs were being held captive, and the distances between each one. I tried to judge just how long it would take me to travel from one to the other. While the Sampsons finished dinner, and then while they were watching TV, I was in my own little world. I thought up an escape plan, step-by-step, minute-by-minute, for rescuing Boomer.

When it was time for Adam to go to bed, I followed him into his room like I always did. I waited for him to fall asleep, and for my chance to slip out and put Operation Boomer into action. I was fairly certain he would fall asleep long before I'd need to sneak out.

At 9:59, I made my move. I quietly stepped off my pillow and went ever so slowly to the bedroom door, which was always left open just a crack. Adam's parents wanted to be able to hear him if he called out in the middle of the night. With my nose, I slid the door open just enough to slip out.

But in my haste, my tail banged against the door. It made a thud. At first, I froze but then I decided to make a mad dash for the back door and freedom. Just as I was squeezing through the doggie door, I heard Adam calling out.

"Rutherford, where are you going? Come back here."

I wasn't sure what to do. I didn't want him to worry about me, but I had to go. I had to save Boomer. I didn't know how much longer he'd be alive. For all I knew, I might already be too late.

I put my head down, sprinted out of the back yard, and never looked back. I was on a mission and nothing could stop me. Adam would just have to trust me. Hopefully, I'd be home in a couple of hours, and all of this would be over.

I knew I'd have no problem finding my way back to the industrial park. Any dog who happens to be part of the hound family, of which I am proud to be a card-carrying member, is known for its amazing tracking skills. Finding the scent that Ace and I had left a week ago was a breeze. I picked it up in no time.

I followed it for a couple of miles, and then, as I neared the dog park, I made a slight detour. It was time to pay a visit to an old friend. It should only take a few minutes, and if I got the kind of cooperation I was hoping for, my rescue effort would be a success.

Phase One had begun.

I got that cooperation, and soon I was back on course and headed to my final destination. When I was about a hundred yards from the outer fence, I could see Ace in the distance. He was waiting for me next to the hole under the fence.

"I was afraid you might not show up," he said as I joined him. "I'm glad you decided to help out these poor, unfortunate victims."

It was hard to keep a straight face. "I wouldn't miss tonight for a truckload of bacon bits," I said.

"I'm glad to hear it. So, tell me, will we be hearing some killer material tonight or just a recycled effort?"

"I'm happy to say that everything tonight is completely original. And I may even toss in a few surprises."

"I can't wait," he said.

Just then, we heard someone coming on the other side of the fence. It was our host, Sledge.

"Welcome back, guys," he said. "Your audience is ready and waiting."

Ace jumped into the hole and squeezed through to the other side. I did the same.

"Is there anything you need for tonight?" Sledge asked. "A water dish, maybe?"

"No, not really," I said. "But I do have a favor to ask."

"You name it."

"Some of tonight's jokes are a little edgier than normal. You know, intended for more of an adult audience. I don't think they'd be appropriate for those little dogs I saw there last week. Is there any way you can leave them home tonight?"

Sledge shrugged. "Sure, I don't see a problem." He leaned in my direction and winked. "Edgier, huh? I like the sound of that."

He turned away and barked loudly. Moments later, two other pitbulls arrived. He whispered something to them. They raised their eyebrows and smiled. I could tell by their reactions Sledge had told them what I had prepared for them tonight. I assumed he had also given them orders to remove the little dogs from the audience.

I smiled. Everything was falling into place.

We followed Sledge across the compound and into the building where I'd be performing. When I walked into the room and entered the ring, there was an immediate roar. It was always nice to have the support of an enthusiastic crowd. I expected they might have a different opinion of me in an hour or so.

When I looked around, I noticed that the room was only about half-full. A number of the big dogs that had been there a week ago appeared to be missing. Then, a couple of minutes later, a large group of them filed in. I didn't think much of it at first, and then I figured it out. Once the little dogs had been escorted back to their cage, it would have taken a bunch of them to move the big rock back in place to keep the little guys from escaping.

Soon the house lights dimmed, and Sledge nodded to Ace. It was show time.

"Can I have your attention, please," Ace said. He waited for the crowd to settle down. "Back by popular demand is the funniest dog in show business. Please give a big welcome to Rutherford, Canine Comic."

I took a deep breath and looked into the eyes of my adoring fans. For some reason, they didn't appear nearly as menacing as they had a week ago. Maybe because I knew they liked me.

But this was no time to get soft. I kept thinking about what Marge had told me about this whole dog-fighting operation, and what happened to the little bait dogs. I had a job to do. I didn't have anything against these pitbulls. I just wanted to save Boomer.

"Good evening, ladies and gentlemen, it's so great to be back."

I had decided to start them out with a series of one-liners.

"Did you hear about the time that Dracula walked into a neighborhood animal shelter and told the staff he was interested in adopting a dog? 'What kind of dog are you looking for?' a volunteer asked. 'Why, a bloodhound, of course,'" he answered.

Rim shot—courtesy of Ace. Followed by laughter. I was off to a good start.

"Hey, I've got a question for you," I said. "When is a black dog not a black dog?" I waited for a response, but there was none. "When it's a greyhound, silly." This time there was applause to go along with the laughter.

"Does anyone out there know what to say to a dog before he begins eating?" The pitbulls shrugged and smiled. "What else but…Bone appetit. Get it? Bone?" They got it, allright. I now had them eating out of my hand.

"Did you hear the one about the mother flea? Her husband found her crying one day and asked her what was wrong. She wiped her tears away and said, 'Haven't you heard? All of our children have gone to the dogs?'" Rim shot.

"You're the best, Rutherford," one of the dogs in the front row yelled out. "Keep 'em coming."

"Hey, tell me this," I said. "What do you get when you cross Lassie with a tulip?" I paused for effect. "Why a collie-flower, of course."

I continued the one-liners for a few more minutes before making the transition to some longer stories.

"Let me tell you about these two families who live down the block—the Parkers and the Taylors. They've been arguing for years, and it all has to do with a dog.

"It seems that Mr. Parker leaves his dog out all day while he's at work, and wouldn't you know it, the dog never stops barking. Finally, one day Mr. Taylor says to his wife, 'That's it. I've had enough. I'm tired of listening to the Parker's dog bark all day.' He then promptly walks out the back door.

"A minute later, he returns with a big smile on his face. 'What are you so happy about?' his wife asks. 'I can still hear the dog barking.' To which her husband replies, "I put the dog in our backyard. Let's see how *they* like it.'"

Ace let out a roar which caused the others to join in.

"I was walking down the street the other day with my friend Gus when he stopped suddenly and said, 'Hey, do me a favor. Wait here just one minute. I gotta do something.'

"I watched as he ran across the street and began sniffing a fire hydrant. When he returned a couple minutes later, I asked, 'What was that all about?'

"'Oh, I was just checking my messages," he said."

The audience members were now on their feet. "Bravo! Bravo!" one of them yelled out.

I bowed a couple of times and waved. Everything was going according to plan. It was now time to put Phase Two into operation.

Chapter 18

Secret Weapon

*I waited for the cheering to die down before making my an-*nouncement.

"Would anyone mind if we took an intermission? I'd like to step outside for a few minutes to get some fresh air. Then, when I come back, I'll be sharing some, shall we say, *grown-up* humor with you."

Needless to say, with the promise of some juicy material, the audience was more than happy to grant my request.

Ace stopped me as I was leaving the stage. "Ten minutes, tops. You're on a roll. You can't keep people like this waiting."

"Don't worry," I said. "I won't be long."

I hurried down the aisle and headed for the exit. On the way, I delivered high-fives to a number of satisfied customers. Once outside, I checked to make sure no one was watching. I had ten minutes before Ace would come looking for me.

I placed my nose to the ground and tried to pick up the scent the little dogs had left when they were escorted back to their cage. I had a pretty good idea where it was, but I wanted the old snout to make sure. It didn't take long. I looked over my shoulder one last time and was off.

I didn't think it would take longer than about five minutes to find Boomer and his buddies. It was dark, though, and nearly impossible to see where I was going. I'd have to rely on scent to find the way.

The trail was rough. I did my best to avoid stepping on broken glass, empty cans, and enough trash to fill a city dump. The people who owned this property sure hadn't taken care of it. It was, in a word, a dangerous mess.

I was about halfway to reaching Boomer when I thought I heard someone calling my name. I stopped and looked around. A moment later, I was just barely able to make out a collie. Wait a minute…it was Marge. What was she doing here?

"Marge? What's going on?"

"I should be asking you the same thing," she said. "I thought I warned you how dangerous this would be."

"I know. But what could I do? I can't just leave Boomer here. I have to try to rescue him, no matter what."

She looked around. "I don't like the look of this place. Let's just get out of here while we can."

"Not unless Boomer's with us," I insisted.

Marge sighed. "I'm not going to talk you out of this, am I?"

I shook my head and smiled. "Hey, how did you find me, anyway?"

"I followed you. Then I waited by that hole under the fence until I was able to work up enough courage to come into this place."

"Now that you're here, why don't you join me?" I said. "We don't have much time. What do you say?"

Marge appeared uneasy. She had made it pretty clear she didn't approve of this rescue operation, but she also knew I would see it through, with or without her.

"Allright," she said reluctantly. "Lead the way."

I picked the scent back up fairly quickly, and we headed for our final destination. A few minutes later, I pointed at the cage with all the little dogs. We could hear them stirring. When we got a little closer, I immediately spotted Boomer.

"Rutherford! What are you doing here?" Then he noticed my accomplice. "Marge? Marge? Is that really you?"

She ran up to the cage, slipped her paw through an opening, and stroked Boomer's head. I was getting a little teary. But I soon caught myself. This was no time to get sentimental. We had a job to do.

"So, now what?" Marge said. "How are we supposed to get him out of here?"

I stared out into the darkness. "I'm looking for my secret weapon."

"Huh?" she said.

"I know he'll come. He just has to. I told him exactly where to find us."

"Who's coming?" she said.

"You'll see." I could feel my heart racing. I closed my eyes and said a prayer. There was little Marge and I could do alone. And to make matters worse, nearly all of my ten minutes had passed since I'd left the roomful of pitbulls.

I was beginning to worry that my "foolproof plan" was a dud. Not only had I put myself in danger, but now Marge as well. Part of me wanted to run away and save my own neck, but I knew there would never be another opportunity to free Boomer. And who knew how much longer he'd survive in this place? We had to act now.

Suddenly, I heard footsteps in the distance. *Oh, no,* I thought. *The pitbulls have gotten wise.* They had figured out my scheme. How could Marge and I possibly defend ourselves against so many?

"Rutherford? Where are you? It's me. Are you around here somewhere?"

From out of the shadows emerged the most glorious sight anyone could have hoped for. It was Jaws. My secret weapon had arrived.

I ran up to hug him. "Jaws! I knew you'd come!"

"Sorry, I'm late. I got a little lost," he said. "Hey, is that Marge?"

"I can't tell you how good it is to see you," she said.

"Ditto," he said. "So, what's the plan?"

"See that rock over there?" I said. "It's blocking a hole that goes under the fence, but the three of us will never be able to move it. The only way in is to go right through the side of that chicken wire cage. That's why I asked you to help."

Jaws licked his lips. "It's just about time for a midnight snack." He grinned. "Where should I start?"

"Anywhere is fine with me," I said. "We just need you to chew a hole big enough for Boomer to squeeze through."

Jaws walked up to the cage and carefully examined it for a minute. Then he winked.

"Piece o' cake." He took a deep breath and chomped down. Phase Three had begun.

"Rutherford, this is a brilliant idea," Boomer said. "Jaws can chew through anything."

I kept glancing over my shoulder. I didn't know how long we'd have before the pitbulls figured out I wasn't coming back. I could hope that they assumed I had gone home. Then again, they'd probably be able to pick up my scent, and once they did, they would follow it to this exact spot.

Jaws had already chewed a hole about the size of a baseball, but he had a little ways to go. Boomer was pint-sized, but he'd never squeeze through such a tiny opening. A minute later, the hole was the size of a softball. We were getting closer.

That was when I realized we were being watched.

"Jaws, hold up a minute," I said. I motioned for the others to remain silent.

"Is this part of your act, Rutherford? To be honest, I don't find it very funny." It was Sledge. He appeared to be alone. He walked up and studied the hole Jaws had chewed. "Nice work."

He turned and walked away to a comfortable distance, like he was planning a quick escape. "I'm afraid I'm going to have to report this, you know." He chuckled. "Did you really think you could get away with it? What'd you think —that you could waltz right out of here with all those little dogs? I got news for you, pal. When I tell the others about this, you'll never get out alive."

I glanced at Jaws. I could see him starting to boil.

"I'll tell you what," Jaws said. "Why don't we settle this right here—you and me. Dog to dog. Winner take all."

Sledge backpedaled. He looked at the hole Jaws had chewed through the fence. By the look on his face, it was easy to tell he didn't want to tangle with that set of choppers.

"I'm waiting," Jaws said. He took a few steps toward Sledge, and then lunged at him.

Sledge turned and ran. And ran. And ran.

Jaws stopped and smiled. "Now for dessert," he said. He walked back to the cage and continued gnawing.

"Hurry," Marge said. "This place is gonna be swarming with angry pitbulls in no time."

After another minute, Jaws stepped back from the cage and licked his lips. "Give it a shot," he said.

"C'mon, Boomer," Marge said, "see if you can fit."

The little Scottie effortlessly squeezed through.

"We did it! We did it!" I yelled. "Now, let's get outa here!"

As Marge, Jaws, and I prepared to head out, we noticed Boomer was still standing next to the cage.

"Let's go, Boomer," I said. "We don't have much time."

Boomer turned and stared into the eyes of the little dogs he was leaving behind.

"I can't do it," he said. "I can't just leave them here like this."

"Boomer, just go," a Pomeranian said. "Don't worry about us. We'll be fine."

But they wouldn't be fine. I knew it, and Boomer knew it. I turned to Marge.

"What do you think? Should we?"

"You're not serious," Marge said. "By the time we get all of those dogs out of there, we'll be surrounded. None of us'll make it out."

"Aw, don't worry about the pitbulls," Jaws said. "I can take 'em."

It was great to have Jaws on our team, but there was no way he could do battle with twenty-five or thirty fighting dogs.

"What do you say, Rutherford?" Boomer said. "Please."

I knew Marge was right. I knew that if we took all of those little dogs with us, it would make our chances of getting out almost impossible. But what could we do? Boomer wasn't going to leave his friends behind.

"Okay, Boomer, they can come with us, but we gotta hurry."

"C'mon, you guys," Boomer said to his former cellmates. "Climb through this hole. It's your only chance at freedom."

And so, one by one, fifteen or so small dogs began squeezing through the hole Jaws had created. You should have seen the looks on their faces once they had made it safely to the other side. They were ecstatic. Some hugged each other. A few nuzzled up to Jaws. And a couple of them thanked me for heading up the rescue operation. Even though we had lost a few minutes, I knew in my heart that we had done the right thing.

I held up my paw and motioned for everyone to be quiet. "Okay, guys, here's the plan. There's a hole under the outside fence about a quarter-mile in that direction." I pointed north. "It's the only way out. I need you to run faster than you've ever run in your lives. Our only chance is to beat the pitbulls there. Got it?"

All nodded.

"Okay, now, I'll lead the way. Jaws, can you bring up the rear?"

"Aye, aye, Captain," he said.

"And, Marge, can you make sure none of our new little friends wanders off along the way?"

"I'll do my best," she said.

I put my head down and began the most important sprint of my life. Every so often, I glanced behind me to make sure our group was still together. No one made a sound, although there was an awful lot of panting going on.

We were about halfway to the way out when I heard barking in the distance. I wasn't quite certain where it was coming from, but as we got closer to the hole, it got louder. Not a good sign. Had Sledge gotten word to the others, and they were now blocking our escape path?

When we had traveled a hundred more yards, my worst fears came true. Along the fence, in front of the hole, shoulder to shoulder, were at least twenty pitbulls.

Part of me wanted to rush them, to bulldoze them, to knock them off their feet. But there was no way I would ever risk the lives of any members of my party—not Marge, not the little dogs, and not Jaws—although he'd probably fare a lot better than the rest of us.

I stopped, and just stood for a moment. My feet refused to move. I wasn't sure what to do. I knew the others were looking to me for guidance.

Then, Marge and Jaws were standing on either side of me.

"I think I could take three or four of them," Jaws said.

"No, I won't let you," I said. "It's too dangerous."

"Maybe I could talk to them," Marge said. "Maybe I could make them see that we're not their enemies—that we're not the ones who force them to live this lifestyle. It's the humans—the bad ones—who are responsible."

"They don't look like they're in the mood for conversation," I said.

I knew I needed to think of something fast. I knew that, at some point, the pitbulls would get tired of waiting for us to make our move. They'd take matters into their own paws and attack.

There had to be another way out. We could try for a section of fence that was unguarded, and ask Jaws to chew a hole right through it. But the exterior fence was made of much thicker metal than the cage. Jaws might be able to get through it—eventually—but there was no way he could do so before the pitbulls were on top of us.

My foolproof plan had failed. We were doomed.

Chapter 19

Watchdog Extraordinaire

I took a look at our enemies, and then at the little dogs whose lives were in our paws. *Think, Rutherford, think.*

I closed my eyes and held my breath. I refused to allow anything to happen to Marge or Jaws or Boomer or...

And then it hit me. Of course. There had to be a gate, somewhere cars would come in and go out. And even if there was a chain of some kind that secured the gate to the fence, all Jaws would have to do would be to gnaw through one link of the chain instead of chewing through a bunch of wires in the fence. We might just pull it off.

"Okay, guys, listen up," I said to the little dogs. "We need to find the main gate for this place. Does anyone remember seeing it?"

They all shook their heads, as did Marge. Jaws appeared to be in deep thought.

"I seem to remember something like that," he said. "When I was lost earlier tonight, I do recall seeing a gate.

I thought I could get in there, but it was locked. Then I found the hole."

"What type of lock was on it?" I asked.

"A chain and a padlock."

"Do you remember where it was?"

Jaws spun around, and tried to get his bearings. "Over there," he said, pointing to his right. "I'm sure of it."

"And do you think you could chew through that chain?" I asked.

Jaws thought for a minute and then smiled. "I'm not sure, but I'll give it a try."

"Okay, big guy, lead the way."

I could only hope the pitbulls would think we'd given up when we suddenly headed back in the direction we had come from.

Jaws and I exchanged positions so that he was leading the way, and I brought up the rear. We went back over the space we had already crossed until he made a sharp left. Within minutes, we were on a dirt road that led us to the main gate. Jaws ran up and examined the chain that held the gates together. He came back with a concerned look on his face.

"Stainless steel," he said. "This isn't going to be easy."

Marge was staring into the darkness. "Did you hear something?

"What?" I said. Then, I heard the faint sound of barking, and it was coming our way.

"Oh, no!" she said. "They're on to us."

Jaws immediately ran back to the gate and began pushing against it. The little dogs appeared frightened—they could sense the danger. Marge tried to keep them calm.

She told them to huddle together. Then she tried to shield them from the oncoming mob.

Jaws ran over. "It's no good. The chain's too short."

"That's okay," I said. "You gave it your best shot."

"Well, it looks like it's up to you and me now, Rutherford."

I felt bad for Jaws. This was all my fault.

"I'm sorry for getting you into this. It wasn't supposed to end this way."

Jaws winked. "It's not over yet, little buddy."

In the shadows, we could now see the faces of our hunters. They pulled up and stopped about twenty yards from us. Some were smiling. Others were salivating. Sledge stepped forward.

"Ready to rumble?" he said.

"Bring it on, tough guy," Jaws said boldly.

It's funny how your life flashes in front of you when you find yourself in a dangerous situation. I thought back to my run-in with the coyotes a few months back. I remember thinking then that my life was about to end. But somehow, I survived. What were the chances, I wondered, of lightning striking twice? Would we live another day? Or was this really the end?

"You know, Rutherford, we may not win this one," Jaws said. "But let's make sure the enemy knows he was in the fight of his life."

Right at that moment, I remembered something my mother had read to me a long time ago. Since I was slower than most other dogs because of my shorter leg, she knew I could end up being a victim if I didn't stand up for myself. She worried about me. So, one day she read a quote to me from someone named Mark Twain.

It's not the size of the dog in the fight, but the size of the fight in the dog.

And remembering that, as if by magic, I wasn't afraid any longer. To be perfectly honest, I was afraid for the pitbulls. They had no idea what they were in for. They were thinking this was going to be easy. Boy, did they have a surprise coming.

I dug in my paws and waited for them to advance.

They charged. I slid over and leaned against Jaws. I could feel him shaking. Or was it me?

Our attackers were moving at full speed, only a few feet away, when they suddenly skidded to a stop. They looked past us to something on the other side of the fence. When Jaws and I turned to look, we saw a half-dozen police cars pulling up with sirens blaring. Their flashing lights illuminated the entire area.

One of the officers got out, opened his trunk, and pulled out the largest bolt-cutter I had ever seen. He ran to the front gate and sliced through the chain, then pulled open the gates and motioned for the parade of patrol cars to enter.

Besides the squad cars, there were other vehicles—a paddy wagon and a pair of animal control trucks. It was as if someone had sent them here, as if they knew exactly what was going on at this place.

The pitbulls scattered.

Most of the patrol cars roared past us, but one stopped. A police officer stepped out and opened the back door. I couldn't believe my eyes when I saw Adam and his dad inside. The policeman retrieved Adam's wheelchair from the trunk.

I ran over to greet them. I jumped up on Adam and began licking him. He was smiling, but it looked as if he had been crying. I guess he was worried about me. I glanced back at Marge and Jaws and the little dogs. They appeared happy and relieved. And who could blame them? Moments earlier, we were all wondering if we had taken our last breaths.

I waved to them. I wanted them to meet my owners. I explained to my friends that it was Adam and his dad who had brought the police, although I wasn't sure how they had done it. But none of that mattered right now. All that mattered was that we were safe, and we were together.

🐾 🐾 🐾

When we got back home that night, or should I say early morning, I overheard a conversation between Adam's mom and dad and discovered how everything had fallen into place.

I knew when I left that Adam had seen me sneak out, but I assumed he would just wait for me to eventually come home. Instead, he and his dad went outside to look for me. When they couldn't find me, they got in the van and drove around the neighborhood. But, of course, I was long gone.

Then Adam's dad remembered the GPS device he'd attached to my collar. So, he checked his phone and saw where I had ended up. He and Adam then followed the directions that took them to the dog-fighting place.

They knew I was on the other side of the fence somewhere, so they waited for a while to see if anyone might show up to let them in. Then, they noticed movement—the pitbulls roaming the grounds. When Adam's dad got a really good look at the dogs, he could see that many of them were in bad shape, and their injuries were consistent with dog-fighting.

That's when Mr. Sampson called the police and reported what he had seen. The rest you know.

🐾 🐾 🐾

A couple of weeks have passed since that fateful night. A lot has happened, and there's still a lot more to sort out. The police arrested six humans who were responsible for running the dog-fighting operation. They're facing fines and jail time.

The pitbulls, once they were all rounded up, were taken to a rescue place that specializes in retraining fighting dogs. I thought at the time those dogs were evil, but the more I learned about them, the more I realized they weren't bad. In fact, they were victims, too. It was the humans—the bad ones—who trained them to fight, and who forced them to live in such a terrible state. If they didn't fight, they didn't eat. I hope they all get the help they need, and someday find real homes..

Then there were the little dogs. The majority of them just needed some TLC. The ones who had been dognapped were reunited with their owners. The others were put up for adoption, and soon found themselves in loving homes. Marge and Jaws, I'm happy to say, were safely escorted back to their respective homes; Adam and his dad made sure of that.

Then there was Ace. As you might guess, he knew all along what was going on behind those fences. He couldn't have cared less about the pitbulls or any of the little bait dogs. He was only interested in his fee. I'm happy to report that the gang at the dog park made it very clear to him he was no longer welcome. He doesn't bother any of us anymore.

That leaves Boomer. When Adam and his dad saw how attached I was to him, and vice versa, they decided to bring him home—just for one night. The next morning, I heard them talking about trying to find a family who might be in the market for a cute little Scottie.

But Boomer, as you might remember, doesn't interview well, so when a possible owner would visit the house to see him, he hid between couch cushions, under the bed, behind curtains—you name it. In the end, it turned out to be the perfect strategy. After a week of failing to find him a new home, Adam proposed keeping him.

I knew his parents would object, so I had my work cut out for me. I taught Boomer how to win over the family. He started paying a lot of attention to Mrs. Sampson. He made it a point to jump onto her lap and snuggle up to her whenever she sat down. Fortunately, he was small enough to do that. And then, whenever it seemed like he had an audience, I would give him a cue to roll over, play dead, shake hands—any number of mindless tricks that tend to impress humans.

It worked. Adam's parents reluctantly agreed to keep Boomer—on a trial basis. But we all know what that means. It was for keeps. Once they went out and bought him his own food and water dishes, and monogrammed pillows, I knew he'd be a permanent addition to the family.

When I look back at the past few months, it's hard to believe everything that's happened. I hope never to find myself in another life-and-death situation. I've had enough of those. Sometimes I think about my dreams of becoming a watchdog. I knew it was a long shot, and then after my accident on the highway, I accepted the fact no one in his right mind would ever adopt me as a family watchdog.

But the other day, I heard Adam telling his parents how brave I was to have risked my life to save all the little bait dogs. That when he and his dad arrived with the police, they found me and Marge and Jaws protecting the little guys from certain death. He then informed his parents that I was now the official watchdog for the Sampson family.

I couldn't believe it. I had actually done it. I could hardly wait to tell the gang at the dog park the next day.

"I gotta give you credit, Rutherford," a German shepherd said. "If anyone had told me that a basset hound with a bum leg could become a family watchdog, I wouldn't have believed it. But when I heard how you led the charge against those fighting dogs and saved Boomer and the others, I just gotta tell you I'm very impressed. In fact, I'd be proud to nominate you for membership in the K-Nine unit at the local police department. My brother works over there, and he's always telling me how they're looking for a few good dogs. Interested?"

"I appreciate the support," I said. "But I think I've had just about enough excitement for a while. Thanks anyway."

And that's how it was wherever I went. It hadn't taken long for word to spread through the dog community about my role in helping bust up the dog-fighting ring. It was even kind of funny. I had worked so hard for so long at trying to find a new career that I had pretty much given up on becoming a watchdog. Now, everyone looked at me differently. They saw me as a watchdog *first* and a stand-up comic *second*.

"Hey, Rutherford," a chocolate Lab yelled one day. "I know you have other work to do now, but would you still have time to tell us an occasional joke?"

I grinned. As much as I was enjoying my new role—official protector of hearth and home—I'll never tire of telling a good joke. I'll always be Rutherford, Canine Comic.

"Hey, did you hear the one about the burglar who breaks into a house looking for loot?"

All the dogs quickly gathered around. It felt like old times.

"The burglar headed for the bedroom and started digging through the dresser drawers. Suddenly, he heard someone say, 'Santa is watching you.'

"He turned around, afraid the owner of the house had caught him in the act. Instead, he saw a parrot in a cage.

"'Santa is watching you,' the parrot said. The burglar chuckled. 'You scared me, bird,' he said. 'Listen, I'm not worried about Santa. He's been leaving me coal for years.' He then went back to his hunt for loot.

"Once again the parrot said, 'Santa is watching you.' The burglar got angry. 'Would you just cut it out.'

"And then from the corner of his eye, he saw the biggest, scariest Doberman pinscher he had ever seen. 'Oh, by the way,' the parrot said, 'I'd like you to meet my friend... Santa.'"

Rimshot. Standing ovation.

It was all good.

END

210

About the Author

JOHN MADORMO is a Chicago area author, screenwriter, and college professor. John's first book, with Penguin Books for Young Readers, was a middle-grade mystery entitled *Charlie Collier, Snoop for Hire—The Homemade Stuffing Caper*, was released in 2012. Book #2, *The Camp Phoenix Caper* and the third installment, *The Copy Cat Caper*, hit bookstore shelves in 2013.

John has also sold a family comedy screenplay to a Los Angeles production company. When he's not writing, he teaches broadcasting and writing courses at North Central College in Naperville IL.

About the Artists

BRAD W. FOSTER is an illustrator, cartoonist, writer, publisher, and whatever other labels he can use to get him through the door. He's won the Fan Artist Hugo a few times, picked up a Chesley Award and turned a bit of self-publishing started more than twenty-five years ago into the Jabberwocky Graphix publishing empire. (Total number of employees: 2.) Most recently, he was named the Artist Guest of Honor for the 2015 World Science Fiction Convention.

His strange drawings and cartoons have appeared in more than two thousand publications, half of those science fiction fanzines, where he draws just for the fun of it. On a more professional level, he has worked as an illustrator for various genre magazines and publishers, including Amazing Stories and Dragon. In comics, he had his own series some years back, The Mechthings, and he even got to play with the "big boys" for a few years as the official "Big Background Artist" of Image Comic's Shadowhawk.

While working as a court clerk in New York state's Unified Court System for more than 32 years years, *STEPHEN TIANO* simultaneously managed to make time to freelance as a book designer and layout artist for 25 of those years. Retiring from civil service, he's continued as a freelance book designer/layout artist and to date has helped bring to press well over a hundred books. All the while, he indulges his love of garlic, mushrooms, hot peppers, and cooking in general.

Stephen lives on the East End of Long Island with his wife Nannette, also an artist working in multiple media and photography, who has learned to live with her husband's tendency to sauté a whole head of garlic with his morning eggs.